Julie Engler

Bo\

Short Stories by L.S. Engler

Copyright © 2012 by Laura Engler
Cover art by Shannon Perry

Find out more about this author and upcoming books at her website, lsengler.com, or follow her Twitter @lsengler

Table of Contents

Acknowledgements

This book is dedicated to my fellow writers and bloggers who have inspired and encouraged me to realize that this dream could become a reality with a little bit of hard work and a lot of support, in particular the whole A Round of Words in 80 Days (aroundofwordsin80days.com/blog) group. It was through my participation with this fantastic collection of writers what I was able to put this book together; without them, I'm not entirely sure it would exist today.

Particular gratitude goes to my beta readers, C. Michael Hubbard, Mike Young, Angela Misri, and Sharon Howard, who saved me from making a lot of silly mistakes and reassured me that people would actually want to read these little yarns. Hopefully, one day, I can return the massive favor they have done me. I'd also like to thank my good friend Shannon Perry for her wonderful work on the cover. Another expression of gratitude is extended to Cameron Chapman for an excellent guide in formatting.

Anyone can write a book, but it takes more than one person to create one. I've shown I can weave together words with some of the best of them, yet the ability to fully express how much I appreciate each and every one of these people completely fails me. Thank you, thank you, thank you!

An Introduction or Acquaintanceship

I haven't the chance to meet L.S. Engler in person, one on one to discuss writerly discussions (or non-writerly discussions, perhaps, something in the key of levitating speculation), but I have talked to her and followed her blog and been given the opportunity to read the stories that follow my little soliloquy, and I can tell you that L.S. Engler is a talented young lady. She's as adept with words as a painter is with hues on a brush, and if a picture is worth a thousand words than a sentence can build a world, and a paragraph a universe, and a book can discover a new religion, and L.S. Engler is blisteringly prosaic in serving up new wonders, old friends, and melancholy miracles.

From her first story, *Dragon Rising*, to her last drop, *The Space Between Worlds*, she gives you enchantment, entertainment, and delightful cognitive inspirations. No, nothing rectilinear or droll in these electronic figures, her prose is inviting without becoming overbearing and deftly cloaks her intentions, drawing you deeper and deeper through the proscenium arch into her worlds (yes, worlds, check out her blog, lsengler.com, and you'll find ubiquitous energy coagulating with hyper-imagination as she fishes through ponds long thought stagnant to deliver magic). It's all here for you to discover, stop listening to me and go find it for yourself, you'll be glad you did.

In short, there's magic to be found here, and I—honestly—wish I had written some the tales you're about to discover. Bravo, L.S., bravo.

--C. *Michael Hubbard,*
20 May 2012

Dragon Rising

Possum, Rabbit, and Prairie Dog had all gone to the river to do the washing, and I had followed to watch them. The sun was bright in the cornflower sky, and hot, so after they had dunked the clothes in the gentle rushing stream, after they had scrubbed and scrubbed and scrubbed, they laid them out on the big flat rocks that had been soaking up the sun's heat. There, the clothes would dry, basking like salamanders, and the girls would splash around in the water themselves, laughing and playing, tossing handfuls at each other until they were drenched and cooled. Then they, too, settled down in the long grass, turned their browned faces toward the sun and soaked it up.

Quiet and still, I crouched next to a boulder too tall and round to be used for drying, underneath a fern for further shelter. I curled my tail in, which was the only way I could prevent it from twitching happily at the serenity of the scene. They had no idea I was watching; the three of them were such pleasure seekers that they had none of the carefulness and caution of their friends, who would have surely caught me. Rabbit was perhaps the most skittish of them, and her bright brown eyes flicked my way on occasion, her pert little nose wrinkling as it tried to pick up the scents carried on the wind. Mostly, though, it was just the sweet grass and the soap still floating by on the river, the fresh linen and the lavender flowers from up the hill.

She looked at me at least three times, straight at me, without seeing me. My ears pressed back with the pleasure of my successful camouflage. The others wouldn't even believe me when I told them that I was peering into the intimate, quiet respite of these three bright-eyed girls, knowledge so valuable that I would instantly be skyrocketed up in their ranks. If only Deer and Fox had laundry duties today! They, out of all the girls in the village, were easily the most eagerly sought after. Next time, perhaps I should try my stealth in the kitchens or the temples to see what other wonderful things girls did when they were alone, but I couldn't imagine anything as splendid as their splashing and laughing, their hair catching in the sun as they tossed it freely around.

And then they began to talk.

"Have you heard?" Possum started, leaning forward to stretch for her toes. Her hair, pale and nearly white in the sun, fell like a curtain, hiding her gentle grey eyes. "There're whispers of a newcomer."

"There are?" Prairie Dog straightened, paying more attention to everything around her, a sharp yet fluid motion that had become a habit of hers; it was as though her spine were made of steel, snapping into place. She drew her hands in close to her chest, another habit. She had cut her hair short that year, a thick sandy bob that brushed against her ears. "Who? Is it the boy with the dark hair? The really big one? Oh, the moment I saw him, I knew he had to be a Bear."

Rabbit smiled, not the shy smile I was used to seeing, but a big one that showed off her two large front teeth without embarrassment. "We haven't had a Squirrel in a while; maybe it's one of those."

But Possum shook her head. "I hear it's a Dragon."

Silence settled over the trio, and my breath caught as well. I was leaning forward, threatening to lose my cover, as my ears pulled forward to hear more.

"There hasn't been a Dragon in ages," said Rabbit, her voice in quiet awe, but I could see she was trembling slightly in fear, too.

"Who is it?" asked Prairie Dog.

Possum shook her head again, before her chin settled on her knees. "Don't know," she admitted. "I didn't hear that part, but Old Wise Eagle and Owl were talking about it the other day. I don't think they saw me, and, if they did, they probably though I was asleep."

Rabbit snorted. "If they saw you, they would think no such thing, Possum. They would have thought you were playing dead, as you always do, and told you to get up and go do something useful."

"That's the whole reason I'm here in the first place!" Possum sunk with a groan. "What a rotten trick. Everyone knows about it, so it never works anymore. I tried it on Coyote, and she laughed so much. What a bi—"

I felt it before they did; in their current forms, their senses were dulled, while mine were sharpened by my animal instincts. I tensed, not knowing what it was at first, but knowing that something was coming, and then I turned my head to see Wolf tearing through the brush and barreling toward the girls. All three of them, each of them natural prey, jumped and shrieked and huddled together in the face of a charging predator; even I had the urge to slink away behind the rock and cower until he was gone. But he began to shift as he ran, his four legs moving smoothly into two legs and two arms, and, only slightly breathless, he stood before the girls with his eyes wild, his long dark hair covering part of his sleek, sharp face.

"Wolf," Rabbit's voice was higher than before, tremulous, as if pleading for the young man not to eat them, though none of us would prey on each other. "What is it? What's wrong?"

"Everything," Wolf huffed. He reached for one of the girls, Possum, who let out a shriek of surprise. She went limp, forcing him to throw his arms around her to keep her from falling as the others two scattered for the cover of a rock littered with skirts. "Come on! We have to—"

"Let her go!" I cried out, pushing forward through one skin, into the other, shaking a little with the transformation as I now stood. Every inch of me was electrified, every hair standing up on end as it would be if I were still in my animal form.

"Cat!" one of the girls, I think it was Prairie Dog, cried out, and, as soon as he saw me, Wolf growled, deep and guttural in the back of his throat.

He chuffed, shaking his head, and he let go of Possum, though a little roughly. "This is not the time to get territorial, Cat," he murmured. "We have to get out of here. We all do. It's dangerous. They sent me here to get the girls; we should return immediately, because odds are someone in a frenzy trying to find out where you've disappeared to, as well."

"What's going on?" Prairie Dog's hands hovered by her mouth, as if that could hold her anxiety in.

"How long have you been there?" Rabbit seemed undisturbed by Wolf's news, her question directed toward me like an arrow, her eyes steady and accusing. I had the decency to blush, but I lifted my chin against her gaze, feeling as though she could look straight through me.

"There's no time!" Wolf barked, and I felt almost grateful for his urgency. "Everyone is gathered at the gates to try to keep the menace under control. We have to go."

"What menace?" asked Prairie Dog, her voice rising in pitch as she moved to cling desperately to Rabbit, whose nose was twitching. I could see that, despite her steady eyes, her limbs were trembling a little again.

"Dragon!" Possum realized with a gasp, and no sooner than the word had passed through her lips, we all heard a terrible sound. I cannot speak for my friends, but I know that it struck me to my very core, and my knees suddenly felt weak. I all but sagged to the ground, and the screeching scream pierced the air again, preceding the great and terrible beast that soared out from the forest and into the cornflower sky.

We all lost it then, feeling that uncontrollable pull in our limbs that brought out bodies into smaller, more compact forms, four legged and furry, the terror rising up in us and pushing us into our defensive state. As my paws touched the ground, I arched my back, every hair on my body fluffing to make myself bigger, my claws ready and digging into the ground. Wolf crouched low and started growling, baring those sharp white teeth that would always snap at me in a fashion he claimed was playful, though I knew better. Prairie Dog managed to find a hole to slink into, as she always did, burrowing deeper to keep herself safe, and Possum's grey body fell with a graceless thump on the ground, her legs stiff and her naked pink tail curled around her as she pretended to be dead, as if that would prevent the monster from noticing her.

Only Rabbit didn't change; she never was nearly as skittish as everyone made her out to be. She stood strong, her hands balled up into fists at her side, staring up at the massive creature circling around them.

Dragon spotted us easily, and I spat and hissed and bounced around helplessly, unable to believe the size of him. No wonder there hadn't been a Dragon in so long! Such a power was too much for one person. He let out another roar, careening through the air and opening his mouth to let out a long burst of flame. The air dried around us, and the clothing on the rocks burst into flame from the sudden scorching. Wolf began to bark maniacally, prancing on his paws, as useless as I was.

And Rabbit continued to stand there, a strange glint in her eye. Dragon was circling, circling, and it was clear that he was about to descend on the one figure that was the easiest for him to grab with his massive, terrifying talons. I let out a yowl of warning, dashing forward ready to leap at her, to do whatever I could to get her down to avoid those reaching claws.

I crouched down low, my bottom wiggling to get me in the right position, and then I froze. Rabbit opened her mouth, and her voice carried strong and sure in the heated air.

"No!" she shouted. "This is not how it's done!"

To everyone's shock and amazement, Dragon pulled back, hovering a moment in front of her before he landed, the mighty force of his wings pushing the air forward. It was clear he was still young, but even in his smaller, still-growing size, he was twice as tall as she. He opened his mouth and let out another shout, like nails scratching down a chalkboard, and it made every inch of my spine shudder. But Rabbit stood strong, shaking her head, despite how close those teeth came to snapping off her pert little nose.

"No!" she shouted again.

"We do not harm our own," she said, softer this time, but still forceful. She didn't break her gaze with Dragon, but I could tell this next part was directed at me. "We must be honest and true and good to each other, even when it goes against our natures. That is how it is, that is how we survive, and that is how it has been for centuries."

Dragon seemed to hesitate, his spined tail flicking in the air, but his wings lowered against his back, and he ducked his head, almost as if in apology. Rabbit smiled, reaching a gentle hand out to his scaled muzzle. "I know," she said, moving forward to embrace Dragon's head against her breast. I felt myself stretching back out into human form, aching more from my envy than from the actual transformation. "It's so strange and frightening at first, but it gets better, I promise."

As she spoke, we weren't the only ones smoothing out into our human forms. Dragon in her arms had turned back as well, and I realized how young and confused he was, just a mere boy, probably not even twelve years of age, and he clung to Rabbit desperately. She eased out his sobs with a gentle hand in his hair, and she glanced up to give us all a rueful smile.

"Let's get him home," she said. "I'm sure the village is in disarray, but there's a lot of work to do. We finally have a Dragon!"

Wolf moved forward before I had a chance to, helping Rabbit along with the boy before he lost control of himself again. I was too dazed to even be sufficiently irritated; I was supposed to have all the quick reflexes, but as they started off, I hung back, feeling useless and marveling all the more over Rabbit.

Possum had only just pulled herself off the ground, dusting the dirt off her skirt as she drifted over toward me. She was shaking her head in disappointment, and she let out a long sigh. "Seriously, Cat," she said, "how long were you there?"

"Oh, shut up, Possum," I said and started following the others. You'd think it would be easy to focus on the fact that we had a Dragon right then, but all I could think about was Rabbit and her soft but steady eyes, and how I would give anything to be a Dragon that day.

Lilacs

Margaret was five years old, and the only people who called her Margaret were her mother and her doctors. Everyone else called her Meg, and she called herself Lilac, after her favorite flower. She thought Meg was mostly a stupid name, unless it was her grandfather saying it, and then it became the best name. Lilac was preferred, though, without a doubt, even if she was the only one who called her that; maybe that was what made it so special. Her favorite game involved pretending to be a lilac, so it just made sense that she should be one, too. There was a thick, unruly patch of lilac bushes growing all around the big back porch of her grandparents' house, threatening to swallow it right up. Margaret would stand in the middle of all those chaotic, twisting branches for hours at a time, perfectly still, until a rogue breeze swept in, and she would sway with the other flowers. She closed her eyes and pictured herself all bristling with small buds, light purple petals, and a thick, heady scent.

She preferred to play this game for long periods of time because the lilacs were only around for about two weeks, then they started to become brown and unimpressive. No one would really notice that she was gone, either; not until a long time had passed, and her grandfather started calling for her, his voice carrying on the wind. She would come running, all the way around the other side of the house so they could never find her secret spot.

But on one particularly sunny, sticky-hot day, her grandmother discovered Margaret there, unexpectedly, while out on her afternoon walk. Margaret's grandmother was a very prim woman, compact and never wasting a single movement if she could help it. So when she stopped her morning stroll to sniff at one of the blooming clusters of lilac, she meant it. She had not meant to discover a round face peering out of the flowers, leaving her startled and surprised. Even her reaction managed to be as quick, small, and efficient as everything else in her life. It went directly to her brain and decided that there would be no more surprises like that on daily strolls, thank you very much. There would be no more daily strolls at all, in fact. The doctors had called it a stroke, and Margaret's mother explained to her that it was nothing at all like what you did in a canoe and that it meant that her grandmother could no longer walk as she used to.

Margaret felt bad about her grandmother, but not so bad that she'd stop playing her favorite game.

It wasn't long after the stroke that Margaret's mother began to take her to see a new doctor. This one called her Margaret like the other doctors, but, unlike those other doctors, this one had a big, wiry moustache like the brush that her grandfather used to polish his shoes. His belly was large and round, like Santa Claus, and his name was utterly unpronounceable. Margaret decided to just call him Doctor Sauerkraut, because that was close enough, and that was what he smelled like, anyway. Every week, she took a trip with her mother and went into a room with a lot of big, intimidating books. She would sit on a large brown couch that smelled old like under the porch. Doctor Sauerkraut would ask her odd questions, boring questions, confusing questions. She didn't understand why anyone would want to know the things that he asked about. Like how she felt when the maid served her breakfast or why she liked lilacs so much or if her mother hugged her often. She began to suspect that Doctor Sauerkraut was not really a doctor at all. He didn't have nice nurse ladies that gave her lollipops, and he never made her stick out her tongue to say "ah" or put cold things in her ear.

Margaret's grandmother was not at all pleased about Doctor Sauerkraut, and she mentioned this to Margaret's mother as much as possible. She called him a head doctor, which didn't seem right to Margaret. After all, he didn't even shine that light through her ears and pretend it went through to the other side. Even the dentist, with all his awful tools on that glistening tray, was more of a head doctor than Doctor Sauerkraut. It was good to know, though, that she wasn't the only one who felt that this new doctor might not really be a doctor at all.

"It's not right," her grandmother would say, shaking her head and stroking the fluffball of a dog sitting on her lap. "Girl that age, seeing a head doctor." It was followed by a lot of things directed at Margaret's mother. Disappointment. Lazy. Negligent. Then she called Margaret a poor girl, which didn't make sense, because they had plenty of money to buy things. Her mother didn't even have to work. She could, as her grandmother put it, just live off the fat of pigs and stay out of trouble, for Chrissakes.

Margaret's grandmother died not long after that, and Margaret always wondered if it was the head doctor that did it, or if it was something else. Her mother muttered her theories under her breath, which meant that Margaret wasn't supposed to hear them, but she did, anyway. Things about just desserts, but Margaret's grandmother didn't bake. Whatever the reason, Margaret started to miss the sound of the wheelchair on the hardwood floors, and she was crying a lot more than usual, too. She just couldn't seem to turn the tears off, like that time she couldn't figure out how to shut off the bathtub faucet. Or like those pretty waterfalls in the Upper Peninsula, just gushing and gushing and never stopping. Her mother had yelled at her and slapped her once, but that didn't make her stop crying, either. It only seemed to make it worse.

It seemed to rain a lot more, as well, making it difficult for Margaret to simply hide under the porch when she started to cry. She began sneaking into her grandfather's library instead, where there were large ladders that rolled along the tall bookshelves and the big, immovable desk that she could crawl under. It was like a small, safe cave. But when she tried it the second time, someone was already there, and Margaret stood still, caught stiff in the act. She wasn't supposed to play in here, and she hadn't realized that her grandfather was sitting in the armchair in front of the black, gaping mouth of the fireplace. The place where her mother had slapped her started to burn with embarrassment and fear, but she just couldn't move her feet.

Her grandfather didn't get upset, though. He patted his knee with a big, slow hand and, dutifully, Margaret climbed up as if he were a jungle gym. He didn't look angry, just very sad, with heavy, drooping shoulders and an odd color to his eyes. None of them spoke, at first, but the tears had stopped. She sniffled quietly as he wrapped his arms around her.

Finally, the time to talk arrived. "Your grandmother," he said, though it seemed more to himself than to Margaret. His voice was deep and crackled around the edges, like a plastic wrapper thrown into a campfire. "Your mother's mother, my wife, is dead, Meg. Do you know what dead means?"

Margaret had to think about it for a long time before she was satisfied with an answer. Her voice was tiny and uncertain when she spoke.

"Dead is when the lilacs turn brown."

"Almost," her grandfather said. "Except for one thing."

"What thing?"

"The lilacs always come back."

She paused, considering. "And Grandmother isn't?"

Her grandfather pulled her closer, lowering his head. "You always were clever, Meg," he muttered into her hair, "in your own way."

Another silence overtook the library, like the shadow of a cloud over the sun. Margaret gingerly rubbed her nose and started to squirm a little, growing restless. Her nose glowed slightly, a dull pink, a faint reflection of her grandfather's dusted red.

That redness became brighter as the funeral neared. The wake was held at the house, which was a little strange, but Margaret's grandfather had a bad knee and complained about the effort involved in going to the funeral home. He held a stubborn devotion to that large estate on the hill, and so had his wife. The backdrop of large windows overlooking the deep blue bay was an effective distraction from the stiff, ashen body covered in black. When Margaret saw the corpse in the open casket and really, really looked at it, she could only stare for a very long time. She clutched at the hem of her dress, wishing that her mother would hold her hand. But she didn't, and they turned around to walk back to the folding chairs in the front row.

"You were very brave not to cry," her mother whispered.

But it wasn't bravery; it was just that she was all dried up by now. There weren't any tears left.

When they reached the chairs, Margaret didn't sit down; she sniffled, ran the back of her hand under her nose, and kept walking forward, gliding fluidly down the aisle between the chairs. Through the entry hall with its dark shrouds over the windows and furniture. Through the door so heavy that she strained to open them. Down the curved stone steps of the porch.

Right into the lilac bushes.

Their short season had already passed. Their purple-blue hue had faded; their sweet fragrance took on a strong note of decay. She fit easily into her small nook, crouching down in her black taffeta dress, staring out at the world. She was a lilac. It was past her season. She was the color of sandy dirt, and she smelled of death.

But she, and all the other lilacs, would get to come back, with time. That made her feel much, much better.

She stayed out in the bushes until it started to rain again.

The Wartburg Incident

"Reason is a whore, the greatest enemy that faith has."
-Martin Luther-

In this grey stronghold, my solitude is heavy and burdensome. The barren halls are so desperate for conversation that they send even the smallest sounds echoing back. The only breath besides my own is the infrequent sigh of Nature stirring the dusty banners drooping from the high ceilings. The fireplaces gape like black, sorrowful mouths, open with hunger for warm, cheerful flames. Only one holds such a turbulent light, but I would hardly call it cheerful. It is the fireplace in my study, in my room, in my prison. My only connection to the world outside is a single window overlooking trees, bare like bones, where not even birds are content to settle.

I am so deeply lonely, though I am not alone. I have a companion, but he is not welcome here. He remains a nuisance, a boor, a torment. He paces, footsteps like clomping hooves clattering on the stone floors, though he appears as a simple, sinewy man in soft bedroom slippers. Every so often, the cold void of his missing shadow passes over me when he leans in close by my shoulder. He hums, thoughtfully, into my ear; it's almost a purr, smooth like his smirk. He reads what I am writing and, as if his mere presence wasn't enough to test my patience, he constantly assaults my intelligence with his inane, simpering commentary. I can only ignore so much.

His soft coo is mocking, and his thin fingers reach out, dancing in the air behind my neck. "Oh," he says, reaching past my shoulder. "That is very good. Almost musical! Do keep it; the rest of what you've written is so dry."

My fist tightens, nearly snapping my quill in twain. I lift the nub from the papers and turn my head to look at him. His angular face is obnoxiously close, and he chooses to ignore my hateful eyes. His smile is malicious, a flash of neat, white teeth, slightly sharp.

"Don't you have a pope to lead around by the nose somewhere?" I try to make my words nonchalant, casually turning away to dip my pen once, twice, a third time into the inkwell before returning placidly to my writing. Perhaps too placidly; I want to completely hide my annoyance, though I know it's impossible.

"It's not the nose I lead him by, my dear Jörg." With a wink, he emphasizes my false name and claps an unwelcome hand on my shoulder. I barely suppress my visceral shudder at his touch. "Besides, he's doing quite well on his own, as you well know."

It has been like this all day, all week, and my anger reaches its boiling point. My hand slaps down on the desk, sending up small clouds of dust into the air. "Fiend!" I lift my voice to match the sharpness of my action. "Why must you insist on bothering me? I have work to do!"

He grins. Of course he does. He's always grinning, and, this time, he even lifts a loose hand to his quirked mouth, as if coquettishly hiding his amused expression. He tucks the other hand close to his chest; it seems as if he's covering a heartbreak until I notice one finger extended, pointing toward my desk, in the manner of a tittering woman bent on gossiping without being noticed. His voice dances. "You will have much more work to do than before," he informs me. "Look."

I am reluctant to follow his finger, my brows lowered in frustrated furrows. I want to be able to decipher what he means without looking, but his face is so impossible to read. I must turn, back toward my desk, where I discover my ink jar has toppled over and a black puddle is slowly flooding over my parchment, drowning my words. I move quickly to pick up the jar, but it's too late, too much is ruined, and a low moan works its way out of my mouth from deep within the pit of my stomach. "And that page was nearly finished!"

"Genesis Eight," he notes, reading over my shoulder again at the few words untouched by the spill. "Of course. Delightful!"

"Go away!" I shout, yanking the parchment off the desk. Black raindrops splatter on the floor. Taking more care, I cradle the ink at the center of the paper and shuffle to the fireplace. The ink has soaked entirely through; what a waste! The flames hiss when I throw it in, a flash of heat and light burning my face. I rub the coarse sleeve of my robe against my cheek, cough in a way that hurts my chest, and slowly return to start a new page. Patience is a virtue. I take my time; it is an interruption from tedium, at least. I sit again with a sigh. "I cannot work like this."

With a deep and rumbling chuckle, he shakes his head. He glides across the room, the tails of his elaborate coat flickering at me like the tongue of a serpent, and then he drops into one of the dusty leather armchairs. He arranges himself lazily, luxuriously, stretching and draping one of his long legs over an arm; his shoulders slouch into the back of the chair. His eyes are sharp as they look at me, watching me write, and one hand twists in the air as he speaks, the other hangs limp between his legs. "Your God," he says, "your Savior, spent forty days in the wilderness with me, without a thing to eat or drink or give Him shade from the hot burning sun, and He could put up with me far better than this. You have the advantage of a nice little castle with a splendid view, correspondence with the outside world, and a larder stuffed with food for your fat little stomach, and already you're fed up with me. I must say, this is so disappointing. Truly pitiful."

"I am far from Jesus Christ."

"All that fuss you gave dear old Leo, Jörg, and here it turns out you're just a petulant little monk. You're so easy that I'd almost consider myself bored with you!"

"If you are so bored," I ask him, "why do you not just leave me be and find yourself more entertaining company?"

His smile is like silk, tempting but cold. "You know me better than that, Jörg. Even if I personally ceased to grace you with my company, I'd make sure you weren't entirely alone."

Those words are all he needs to inspire sudden flashes of the imps that had been tormenting me. Garish trolls that steal away my writing utensils and shred my parchment, wretched succubae that writhe suggestively on the ink-splattered rug. They manifest in the study, clear yet transparent apparitions pulled from the recesses of my consciousness and the darkest depths of hell. All the grotesque tools in his sinister arsenal, on display to remind me that his influence has a tight hold on these empty halls. I firmly shut my eyes against them, giving my trust to faith to guide my hand as I continue to write. I push my pen across the blank page, my lips moving with commitment as I recite Latin prayers for my blind German scribbling.

I feel something tug at my pen, so I tighten my grip. I open my eyes to an unholy tempest fluttering my pages, but I smack my hand down again to hold them all still. I remain focused on the words and the words alone: laboriously dancing in careful script, they provide a sturdy anchor against the spinning storm of demons around me. The candlelight flickers and the fire in the hearth falters, causing the room to drop into a sharp, bitter cold. But I continue still, warmed instead by the blaze of my letters. He was right about them, my words. They are musical, bold and triumphant, drowning out the shouts and screams intended to distract me. I focus on the words. The world around me drops into an unnatural darkness, impregnable night spreading over the study, but I can still see as if my words create illumination in their transfer from mind to matter. The light surges back, blinding now, but I still write. I focus on the words.

I am sweating profusely through my robes, and my jaw hangs, slightly slack, as if that could make breathing easier. I am not sure if this invading heat is from my driving inspiration or if it is from the twisting, reaching spires of hellfire springing up around me from the floor, the walls, the ceiling. Cold hands with digging claws pull at me. In my ears, shrill voices scream untold terrors. I brush them off as one does flies, and I keep writing with defiance, chanting the lines as I translate them, singing them, heralding them into bold proclamation. The raucous noises rise to the metronome of my scratching pen while they increase their ferocious attempts to distract me. I scream out, possessed with their psychotic rhythm, matching my pace to theirs until I feel myself rising to my feet. I am standing, my arms pushing them away. Amid the thrashing and swatting, my hands find the small jar of ink.

My body moves on its own accord. My right arm bends back over my head, behind me, fingers tight around the clay vessel. A drop of ink falls to my shoulder. I shout something, the language familiar, but I do not know the words, and my arm pushes forward, straightening as my fingers fly open. The jar leaves my hand, sailing over the sea of stricken demons sprawled out on the floor. It races straight for him on the other side, in his chair, his eyes wide with shock. He leans back just enough to avoid the jar, and it shatters against the wall behind him. A dark stain drips on the stone like black blood.

"I asked you to leave me alone," I inform him once I find a breath of air. "I have work to do."

My neck hurts from how tightly I've been holding my jaw, and I stretch to out to relieve the pain. I brush the lingering remains of dissipating devils from my sleeves with defiant importance and then, calmly, I sit back down. I straighten my papers. I clear my throat and find a new jar of ink.

He stares at me for a good, long moment. I am certain he does not know what to think, but I will pay it no mind, I will just start writing again. By the time I reach the bottom this new page, he begins to laugh, rich and full, grating on every one of my tense nerves.

"Good show, Martin!" He calls me by my proper name, though I do not know if he does it out of respect or merely to mock me. I force myself not to care. "Your convictions are certainly strong, I must give you that. You'll cause me quite a bit of trouble in the future, I can feel it! But I look forward to it. I enjoy a challenge, and I was so worried you were just a wet blanket, my friend."

I want to tell him that I am not his friend, but I ignore him instead, devoting only a corner of my attention to watching him as he begins to move. He stands with immeasurable grace, mimicking me by brushing off his sleeves. As he takes his slow and deliberate steps toward the door, I feel suddenly troubled. All that, and now he stalks away because I threw an ink jar at him? There is something more here, but I do not know what, and it troubles me greatly. But what more can I do? I don't look up. I dip my quill once, twice, a third time.

"I know you are not leaving just because I want you to," I say, as coolly as I can manage.

"Of course not," he replies, his smirk betrayed by the red sheen in his eyes. "I've only just remembered that I have so many others to torment. You didn't think you were so special I'd spend all my time with you, did you? I've an appointment with a pope. But don't despair, my dear Martin Luther. I won't be long, and I'm never too far away."

Flesh and Feathers

The fog was descending, creeping in from the mountains and cloaking the lake in heavy mist. Birgitte pulled the heavy wool blanket tighter around her shoulders, looking up at the darkening sky, and she smiled. "We should probably be heading in soon," she said, though her wistful voice betrayed her and made it clear that she wanted to stay, that she could stay forever. "It will be night before we know it, and there's sure to be some talk or trouble if we're too late."

Sitting across from her in their little boat, Ian leaned forward with a grin. He gently pushed on the oars, propelling them smoothly across the lake. "I'm not worried about a little bit of talk," he said, "are you?"

"I suppose that all depends on what they're saying," Birgitte smiled back, fluttering her eyelashes, though she doubted Ian could see them very well in this gloaming. "I can't imagine it would be anything my father would like to be hearing."

Ian's hearty laugh echoed against the low mountains and the thickening fog. "There's a fair point," he allowed, "but I'm afraid I can't go in yet, Birgitte. I've yet to see my selkie."

"Your selkie?" Birgitte asked, her eyebrows lifting with skepticism, though her voice remained as warm and bright as the sun sinking slowly down the other side of the mountains. "I was not aware that selkies could be claimed as someone's own. Quite the opposite, as a matter of fact. I can't imagine a seal who turns itself into a beautiful woman is very interested in mere humans owning them."

As she spoke, a long, lonesome cry drifted through the air; the fog made the sound seem close and terribly intimate. A black bird burst through the mist, flapping its wings and letting out the call again, coarse and rough from his yellow beak. After spiraling overhead, it landed on bow of the boat, fluffing its wings. It affixed its beady black gaze on the two of them, releasing an accusing noise.

"Look," said Birgitte, quietly. "A crow."

"Go on," Ian said, frowning at the bird. He waved a hand at it, to spook it off. "Get."

"Ian, don't. It's just a wee birdy."

"A wee birdy? Birgitte, that's a crow."

"What of it?"

"Everyone knows they're harbingers of bad news. Get! Go on!"

With a loud objection, the crow glared at Ian before beating its wings and taking to flight. Its mournful bleating carried it away, long after it had been swallowed up by the fog. Birgitte turned her head to watch it disappear, her shoulders sagging with sadness. "Selkies," she said, "crows as bad omens. When did you become so superstitious, Ian O'Connell?"

He didn't answer at first, letting the steady pace of his continued paddling answer for him. If there was a storm approaching in the mists, it was now mirrored on his face as he studied Birgitte carefully. When he spoke, his voice was quiet. "If I tell you," he said, "will you kiss me?"

Birgitte's tongue brushed lightly over her lower lip, before she bit it with uncertainty. "What if I was planning on kissing you anyway?" she asked.

His grin was crooked and uncontrollable. "Then all the more bonus for me."

"Alright, then, tell me."

"Kiss me first."

"Ian O'Connell!"

"Kiss me, and I'll tell you whatever you like, anything at all, just grant me that one pleasure before I lay my soul open and vulnerable to you, Birgitte Aubersohn."

She knew to hesitate, not to be too eager, and she had the decency to blush and duck her head before giving her quiet agreement. She leaned forward, closing her eyes. Her lips found his easily, as if they were drawn to each other, and a happy sigh escaped them both. He brought a hand to her cheek; her fingers brushed through the rust-colored curls on his head.

Somewhere, the crow cried out again, but they barely noticed it. They pulled away once they realized they were losing their breath; they found it difficult to catch it again even after they'd separated, staring wistfully at each other in wonder of the feelings rushing through them.

"Well?" asked Birgitte once she felt the heat cool from her face and her head wasn't swimming so much.

It was Ian's turn to hesitate, his turn to bite his lip with nervousness. "I saw one's skin," he said, finally, lifting his chin in resolution. "A selkie's skin, on the shores of this very lake. I thought it might be something else at first; it made no sense, but it looked like a wet wool blanket, all abandoned and crumpled up, discarded and unwanted. But when I got closer, when I actually got to touch the thing, there was no denying it. That was seal's skin there on the shore, tough and brown, and there were no cuts or anything, like it had just been shucked right off and that was the end of it. Pity, the selkie clearly wasn't hanging around. But there's got to be selkies in this lake, I'm sure of it. How else would you explain away something like that? You just can't."

Birgitte sat as though a steel rod had been forced into her back; she stared at Ian with eyes wide and round as the very moon hiding behind the mists on the lake. Ian regarded this expression with regret and worry, his brow furrowed with concern.

"I think you should take me back, Ian," she said quietly. "Drop me off the shore now, if you please, I should like to go home."

"You think I'm right mad, don't you?" he despaired.

But she shook her head, golden curls bouncing. "No," she said, making it firm, making it convincing. "I would just like to go home now. It's late, Ian, my father will worry, you know he will. But, well…perhaps you're right, about the crow. It's a bad omen to be seeing crows on a night like this, Ian, and…"

She paused, looking down at her hands in her lap, at the knots being made with her fingers. "I've seen them, too," she whispered softly.

"You have?"

"I have. But, please, talking of such things on this sort of night only stirs up mischief and trouble, Ian. Drop me off. We can talk about this in the morning."

Though it clearly pained him to do so, Ian nodded and agreed to take her back. He started to row the boat again, moving in silence toward the still bright and sandy shore. When the boat stopped, Birgitte carefully extracted herself from within, thanks to the aid of Ian's hand. Feet on the shore, she leaned forward to kiss him again, something long and gentle to last him on his trip back across to the other side of the lake.

Ian made his parting words with a smile, looking up fondly at the pale figure in front of him. He pushed off into the water, drifting away smoothly. "I believe I'm going to marry you one day, Birgitte Aubersohn," he told her.

She gave him a soft, wan smile back. "I've no doubt you will, Ian O'Connell."

Birgitte watched him as he paddled away from her, the rhythm steady, until he disappeared into the fog like the crow. She waited a moment more before she could breathe again, the tension slipping out of her like a fish slipping under the surface of the water. She carefully made her way off the white sandy shore, across the shiny black stones, around the corner of a tall outcropping, and she nearly sobbed to see that the skin, like a wet wool blanket that someone had just left behind, was still there. She rushed to it, scooping it up into her arms and holding it close, drawing in the familiar scent of herself and, now, of Ian. She stepped out of her clothes, of her white dress and her soft shoes, folding them carefully and tucking them into a crevasse created by wind and time.

She stepped into water with the skin and ducked underneath the surface, where it would be much easier to slip in. She did a dance with herself, with the water, smooth and graceful as her human limbs and her human features merged and morphed and the seal dove down quickly, into the depths and out toward the sea. At least until morning. At least until the crows were at rest.

Swing

Tobias first saw his target's house from across the street, and it made him want to just turn around, march back into Garfalion's office, and refuse every beautiful cent of his dirty money. He didn't have a problem killing a man in cold blood if it was deserved, but there was a whole lot more here than what was given in the job description. Maybe it was the white picket fence, separating one toy-littered patch of green lawn from another. Or perhaps it was the clothesline, old-fashioned but energy conserving, stretched from one rectangular window to a telephone pole and decorated with an assortment of colorful and varied garments. It could have even been the orange and white cat of a particularly fluffy nature sunning itself on the concrete stoop.

But, deep down, Tobias was pretty sure what got him in the end was the swing. Rudimentary and simple, it was little more than a thick board flanked by thick ropes, hanging from the thick tree sprawling over most of the tiny yard. It swayed slightly, as if from recent use or a gentle breeze. Just a simple swing, nothing extraordinary, but it managed to cause a seizure-like twitch in his right arm. The line where his thick hair met his dark skin was damp with sweat as faint memories of laughter bubbled up in the corners of his mind. Phantom figures of healthy young boys, taunting each other as they circled the swing with boundless energy. Spirits of the past, slipping into the present. Tobias closed his eyes tightly until he could burn the images out. He couldn't do this.

***

"I can do this," Tobias said, giving the papers in his hand another glance, the photographs, the profiles, the details. They were all things that bordered on interesting, but they remained relatively common fare, making the job seem almost too simple. "In fact," he looked up, allowing a ghost of a smile to grace his lips, "I'd be honored to complete a mission for such a highly esteemed company." He slipped the information back into the large envelope and sent it skittering across the heavy desk.

It came sailing back, its contents nearly spilling onto the hardwood floor. "Keep it," Ophedius murmured, a sneer deepening the scar on his fleshy cheek. "You may need it. And cease the flattery. You're coming off as desperate."

Tobias cleared his throat. He was desperate, everyone knew that, but he wouldn't apologize for it. It was like denying that your jacket was wet during a thunderstorm.

Ophedius stood, the heavy chair that matched his heavy desk sliding back easily; he pulled at the cuffs of his stiff jacket as he approached the large glass windows looking out over the lights and shadows of the city. As

Ophedius spoke, Tobias could see his reflection against the midnight background, a young man with very old eyes, searching the metropolis carefully.

"You know, Gainswellow," he said, lifting his chin, "we've been keeping a very close eye on you lately. I would advise you to do your best, but you were planning on doing that anyway, weren't you?"

Holding in his irritation at the snide sarcasm, Tobias just kept his smile steady, his voice pleasant. "I couldn't imagine doing anything else but my best for you guys," he said. "I assure you, you won't be disappointed."

Ophedius hummed thoughtfully as he fixed his tie, black with red speckles on it like bloodstains. "I certainly hope not."

He turned back, satisfied with the adjustments, and gave Tobias a cool nod of his head. "Unless you have further questions on the mission, Gainswellow, I must ask you to leave now. I have a great deal of pressing business to attend to."

Tobias returned the nod, more stiffly and quickly than he would have liked, and stood. He took the envelope in one hand, Ophedius's hand in the other. "Of course," he said. "Ophedius, thank you. Always, it's been a pleasure."

The lie made him stiffen his back as he turned around stepped out of the office.

***

Tobias stepped into the library, trying to keep them soft, but it proved to be a difficult task. The silence of the library amplified each footfall. He knew that was what Silver liked that about it, among many other things, but it disquieted Tobias. Silver sat ahead of him, at one of the desks, and he lowered his book as he looked over his shoulder. He smiled faintly, placing a thin piece of paper into the book to mark his page. The chair squeaked as he swiveled around to greet Tobias.

"Hello," he said in a hushed, library-appropriate tone.

"Figured I'd find you here," Tobias said, looming over the other man, who leaned back in his chair to look up at him. "I need you to do some research for me."

Silver beamed, pushing his ill-fitting glasses up the bridge of his large nose. "Good! I was wondering when I would have an actual reason to be here. What do you need?"

Tobias reached for a chair, pulling it out from the table before dropping smoothly into it. His long legs stretched out underneath the table, but he leaned forward imploringly. "I'm at a crossroads, Silver. I've got this job, but there's a problem. Whenever I find myself there to complete the task, I just…"

He trailed off, frowning as he fought to find the right words to describe it. Silver arched one of his prematurely grey brows. "You just what?" he prompted.

"Freeze," Tobias said after another moment. "Seize up. Spaz out. I just can't do the job."

Silver hesitated with his response, so Tobias rushed to fill in the space. "I need you to find something out for me," he said. Propelled by his anxiety, he stood, already abandoning the chair and running a hand through his hair. He pulled out the thick envelope from his back pocket and threw it on the table in front of Silver. The other man eyed it warily.

"All you'll need should be in here," Tobias continued. "Do everything you can to find out why a man like this would be involved with Leo Garfarlion. I know we're expected to act without question or prejudice, but it... this is different. You have to help me figure it out."

Silver reached over and placed a hand over the envelope, pausing he pulled it closer. "No problem," he said, eying his new assignment with a blend of curiosity and concern.

"Yeah," Tobias grunted, shaking his head and voicing what he imagined Silver was thinking. "I know. There's not a single thing on this planet that would make hesitate to finish a job, but that envelope apparently contains the impossible."

***

The impossible task of avoiding the shadows in the hallway had become a little less so, so as long as Tobias took his time and paid very close attention to every step he took. He remained in the squares of light along the hallway, which kept him safe, but he was terrified of even one misstep. Both his hands were wrapped around his gun, a single, shaky finger poised over the trigger. Bullets wouldn't kill it, Silver had said, but they would at least earn Tobias some time, enabling him to execute what needed to be done to kill it. Silence surrounded him, punctuated by the persistent presence of a ticking clock. Slow and steady like paced footfalls, reminding him that timing was everything.

Every second was heavy with fear. Every shift in the large pools of dark shadow around him caught both his eyes and his breath, and he had almost fired at nothing several times. He scolded himself for his nervousness, sharply repeating a reminder that this was more than just a matter of completing a job. This was more than just getting in good with one of the most notorious and successful con men in Analisia City. This was a matter of life and death.

***

Life and death, but it was never quite that simple. When dealing with head honchos like this, they always insisted that things be done with style, with finesse. Ophedius had explained it simply to Tobias: make it tragic, make it shocking, make it memorable. The tragedy aspect of it was emphasized, and that's why the house had been such an ideal place for the assassination. But Tobias just couldn't do it. The white picket fence. The clothesline. That bloody swing. The scene was all too familiar, taking him back to a life before he had to depend on his gun.

Thankfully, the house was not the only potential setting for tragedy. This second setting gave him the chance to set it up to look like a suicide. And Ophedius be damned if that wasn't good enough. At least he would be dead, and Tobias could at least seem to be blameless.

The target worked in a building with poorly lit hallways. Scheduling an appointment had been easy. The vaguely attractive secretary with swinging hips led Tobias into a tidy office, dark from only one window and low lights. Before the large desk were two chairs of black leather, and Tobias sunk into one. His eyes scanned sterile walls, plastered with pictures alternating between works of art and the faces of his family, beaming smiles from three children, in portraits or photographs capturing the memories of first days of school, birthday parties, and dance recitals. Two girls, twins it seemed, and a boy, with a mop of blonde hair. He glanced over them mildly, reminding himself not to pay attention to any detail that would give the target personality and humanity. Eventually, his focus almost settled on one with the swing in it, the three children gathered around it, but the door opened and pulled him away before it could take effect.

"Ah, Mr. Smithe, I assume?" The target smiled, moving across the room in a casual stride. He kept one hand in his pocket while the other extended toward Tobias. Just like in the picture from the envelope, he had a very unassuming face, gentle eyes hidden behind small, stylish glasses, blonde hair, much darker than his son's, brushed back neatly against his head. Tobias had never been assigned to take out someone like this before, so clean-cut, so average. As soon as their handshake ended, Tobias settled back into the chair and his victim settled into the one behind his desk. "It's good to meet you, and to have this opportunity! Dolores says you have a very interesting proposal for me and my business?"

The fingers on Tobias's left hand twitched, his jaw clenched. What a perfect opportunity to present his Onyx Titanium gun and put it to use. Glorious, properly dramatic, and it could be quick and dirty, but he just couldn't get his fingers to grasp the hilt to pull it out of its pocket. Those soft faces staring at him from the wall, the pieces of innocence and happiness. He could hear their laughter, the sun dappling on the grass as it came through the tree over the swing, and he couldn't do it. He had to close his eyes against his own memories.

"Is everything okay, Mr. Smithe? Are you ill?"

Tobias realized he was gripping the side of the chair and his breathing was labored. And he was sweating again. Forcing out a cough, he shook his head, carefully attempting to regain his composure. "I... I'm sorry," he gasped. "I don't know what's come over me." Feigning a little bit of a struggle, he flashed the most convincing smile he could muster and dove right into the false proposal that he and Silver had fabricated in the event that he couldn't pop the guy off right away. The target listened intently to Tobias's ramblings, oblivious to the fact that Tobias really had no idea what he was talking about. "So you see, it could be quite simple," he concluded, vaguely. "Perhaps...we could meet at another time to discuss this further, after you've had a chance to digest it."

"How very intriguing!" the target said, leaning back in his chair with a pleased laugh, a look of eager excitement on his plain face. "I would like to explore this in further detail, Mr. Smithe, yes. Wouldn't it figure that I'm booked solid today? I know it may sound like an off time, but would you be available to meet me here tomorrow night, say, around eight o'clock? That would fit into my schedule perfectly, give me some time to bring a few of my own ideas to the table?"

It did sound like an off time, that was true, but Tobias figured that could work to his advantage. He nodded, giving a lopsided smile as he stood up. "I'm just glad you had the time to see me today," he said blithely. "I think eight sounds good."

***

Nothing that Silver had to say sounded good. The library was still dark, still quiet, and he had been waiting for Tobias, going over the information over and over again. Even in the shadows around them, or perhaps because of them, Silver's face looked luminously pale, the mirth drawn out of his expression, replaced with a deep concern that had Tobias frowning the moment he saw his friend.

"What have you found for me, Silver?"

Silver hesitated, sighing as he leaned back in his chair. "Well," he said,fixing his glasses gone askew, "as you asked, I did as much research on this guy as I could. At first, all I could find was what you had provided me with, all the usual data and information, but then I stumbled on something... something both amazing and terrible, Tobias." He shook his head, staring down at the gathered research, like he was afraid it would jump up and bite him.

"What is it?" Tobias could feel Silver's distress creeping through the air, leeching into his own skin. "Does it have anything to do with Garfarlion? Ophedius?"

"Tobias." When those eyes looked up, Tobias almost shuddered from a chill, despite the thick sweater he wore. "I don't know how to put this. But this man... you're going to have a hell of time killing him, considering he's already dead."

"Dead?" The shock he felt was kept under careful control; Tobias only lifted an eyebrow. "What are you talking about, Silver?"

"An official obituary was never released," Silver explained, "and there's an incomplete medical document regarding his death. Apparently though, , his body just disappeared from the morgue, and our wonderful health care facilities were too busy to concern themselves with what might be just another corpse robbery."

"No." Tobias stared at Silver. "He can't be dead, that's absurd. I was just talking to him yesterday. You knew that. And I'm scheduled to meet with him in about an hour, too, with that crazy business plan you cooked up."

Silver took off his glasses, rubbing his eyes, and when he replaced them, he looked tired and haggard...and afraid. "The man you are meeting," he started slowly, carefully, "is not the man that you think he is. It's the same body of the man you think he is, but there's something else inside, Tobias. I honestly didn't think they really existed, no one does, they're fairy tales, children stories, but it's the only explanation. You can't go to this meeting, Tobias. Just don't go, and forget this mission entirely."

"Are you insane?" Tobias smacked his hands down on the table, leaning in with a burning glare. "I have to do it! If I don't, I'll have Garfarlion's henchmen on my tail! You don't agree to a Garfarlion job and just back out of it, Silver, not if you want to stay alive."

"What we're dealing with here is much worse than anything Leo Garfarlion could do to you," Silver said. "Listen. When they found your man's body, they found another decayed, deteriorated body, belonging to a prominent doctor who had recently stepped out of surgery being performed on your man. This is the case of a shadow stealer, Tobias! It had transferred itself from the doctor's body to your target's. It needed to seek a new body because it was becoming too difficult to maintain the last, and the surgery gave him the best chance."

Tobias blinked, choking on a reaction stuck in his throat. Shadow stealers. Evil little daemons of legend that would hide in the darkness until they could kill a man and take over their body. From there, it was said that the creature would gain energy from those around him, figuratively sucking away their souls. But they were just stories. Myths. They couldn't possibly exist, and yet…as he stared at Silver searching for some sign of a cruel joke, it was all starting to make sense. The darkened hallway, the strange hours, the white picket fence. A long groan, like death, slipped out of him. "You've got to be kidding me."

"Just don't do it, Tobias. Please. It's too dangerous."

But Tobias shook his head, straightening up from the table. It wasn't just the dim lights in the library casting the grim shadow over his face. "No," he said. "I have to. Now more so than ever, I have to do this."

His dark eyes focused on Silver with immovable determination. Silver knew that look, and he knew that there was no chance of changing his mind. He nodded, his reluctance palpable. "Fine," he said. "Just... be careful."

***

Carefully, Tobias walked the line of light down the hallway toward the office door. His right hand reached for the doorknob, almost slipping from the perspiration lining his palm. Taking in a deep breath, he turned it, gave it a gentle push, and the door slowly swung open.

A square of light fell into the darkness of the room, Tobias's tall silhouette etched into it as he stepped forward. It...the target, the shadow stealer, whatever it was...knew that Tobias knew what it was, and it had prepared itself for his arrival. In the quiet of the evening, in the darkness of the room, he could hear it moving around, like a whisper, but he couldn't find even a small sign of the demon. Tobias took a step back, so his shadow didn't merge into the others. He reached for the light switch on the wall, but pulled back as if burned by the edge of the shadow. The switch was on the wall within the room. If he so much as put a finger inside the darkness, the creature could take him. He pulled a small flashlight out of his pocket.

The circular disk of illumination jerked around the room. A limp body was collapsed across the desk; already, the creature had abandoned his old skin in anticipation of a new one. Every so often, a dark spot would appear on the edge of the light, and a small whimper would fill the room as it skittered away. It was so quick that Tobias couldn't keep the light on it long enough. If he could, he could incapacitate it, and it would be easier to kill.

He held his gun erect beside his head as he took another step back, flashlight brandished in the other hand. "Why don't you come get me?" he called, falling into taunts. "Why waste your time? I know that each second you spend outside of a body, you grow weaker. Well, my body's pretty strong, and young, and I have a position of influence in this world, too. That's what you want, isn't it? That's why you're working with Garfarlion, right? Make a deal with him to find you bodies. I have to admit, that's pretty smart, take a family man. Access to the boundless energy of children. You must be incredibly strong by now. But you're getting weaker. Take me now, show me the strength you gained from their innocence. That is why I was sent here, wasn't it? To be your next body?"

There seemed to be a hiss of reply, but it could have been nothing more than the air conditioning unit kicking into gear. Tobias waited, his jaw set tightly to keep from shaking with the tumultuous fear inside him. He knew the challenges wouldn't work. The creature would just stay there as long as Tobias did. He sucked in a breath, holding it to steel him with enough faith to turn around, exposing himself for the perfect opportunity for the shadow stealer to attack.

It was a gamble, a risk, but so was everything else in life. Just mere seconds after he turned away, he spun back around, firing the Onyx Titanium into the darkness with resonating shots. Inhuman, squalling wails responded, as the bullets disappeared into the black abyss of the shadow stealer. It fell from the surprising impact, right into the square of light from the door. For good measure, Tobias released a few more shots. Although the thing was already convulsing and hissing as its death pains rattled it, he figured he'd better make sure.

If he had been second slower, he would have been dead. The twitching stopped, the shadow seemed to bleed into the carpet, the light seemed a little less bright than before, and Tobias let out a sigh. He couldn't believe it worked. Exhausted, he dropped the flashlight at its feet, and he turned again, this time leaving for good, but not until after he flipped on the light switch in the office and let the door slowly swing shut.

***

The swing hung from the large willow tree on the hill, thick ropes keeping it up and blending in with the long, draping branches. A private little paradise, bothered only by the intruding specks of sunlight that watched the two boys take their turns, laughing and challenging the other's ability to touch the canopy with the tips of his dirty sneakers. Jeers about failing to land on your feet after you took flight and chants about girls not being allowed. The grass stains on their trousers were deeper than philosophy, their hair messier than religion.

They barely noticed the shadow against the thick trunk of their sheltering tree. Of course, they knew she was there, but they had more important matters to attend to, like perfecting that flip over the thick wooden seat. It was probably for the best that they didn't acknowledge her beyond an absent little, "Mum, look what I can do! Hey! Mum!" If they bothered to see that there were tears in her eyes, tears down her cheek, they wouldn't know how to respond. They wouldn't know what to do about the letter she held in her hand, pulled from a plain, nondescript envelope. But the moment they saw the vacant look in her eyes, they would ask. They would want to know what happened, what was making their mother cry. And she would think of a way to explain it to them, in the private little paradise of their swing playground. "Trevor. Tobias. Your father... he's dead."

The Truth and Lies of a Body in the Snow

We found the body in the snow at precisely 8:57 p.m. I remember because I was watching the clock tower, hoping to see it turn over to nine. We gathered around the figure, awestruck, uncertain of what to do. Christian suggested that we bury it. Mary was set on leaving at that instant to tell someone. Gabe wanted to have sex with it, but we told him no.

Such serene beauty, bare blue skin like the sky on a washed-out morning. Its dark, purple lips were parted as if it were still breathing, but there was a definite stillness to its chest. Pale, white hair cascaded over its small breasts as if modesty was a great concern in death, though tiny erect nipples still pushed through in defiance. Its eyes were shut, so it almost looked like it was just a woman, taking a nap in a chilly bed. I wondered out loud if that might be the case, that maybe it was just sleep, but my thoughts were met with instant contempt.

"Asleep?" Mary grunted, her sneer cutting through the frosty air. "In the snow? Don't be stupid, Alice. Let's just get out of here; let's go tell someone, and the cops can deal with it."

She didn't wait; her words were followed by the crunching of snow beneath her boots. The others also started to turn and depart. Not quite ready to leave yet, I stood marveling over how quickly they could abandon the body. The idea that it was just sleeping compelled me to stay. I stared intently, waiting for that moment when it would stir with a heavy breath of slumber, revealing itself to be alive after all. When the others realized I was just standing there, they called my name, like calling a dog, but I ignored them. I had to see. I had to check for sure. I had to reach out for it, touch it, let my fingers discover the truth.

My fingers trembled with nervous twitches as they slowly reached for the smooth skin of its cheek. The ghostly breath from my mouth billowed up into the frigid air and quickly disappeared. I forced the hard lump in my throat down to the bottom of my red rubber galoshes. Only inches more and I would know for sure if its skin was warm with life or as cold and dead as everything that surrounded it. Just a little bit more.

What happened next occurred so quickly that it could have been mistaken as not happening at all. But I know, deep down, that it did. Right as I was about to caress that cheek, the dead eyes flung open, big and black and cold. They pierced into me like daggers of ice, and a freezing hand snatched my wrist; I could feel it even through my thick winter coat. I shouted, surprised, terrified, shocked, staggering backwards as I yanked my arm free.

As quickly as it had grabbed me, it let me go. The black marbles of its eyes rolled back into its head. I fell into the arms of my siblings. They dragged me away as I stared in horror at the body.

It looked just as it had a second ago, undisturbed and unmoved. But the movements were so bright and vivid and terrifying in my mind. I realized that it had whispered words, the purple lips parting and the fog of a breath reaching my ear. It had pulled me in to whisper my name, and it had asked for my help.

***

Breakfast the next morning was a fog as I pushed a spoon idly through the mush of cinnamon oatmeal. I stared at my wrist, wondering why I couldn't see a mark, though I could feel one, the icy burn of its grip like an invisible bracelet. I hadn't slept that night, haunted by visions of the strange creature in the snow. That face, with its inhumanly dark eyes, filled with intense pain. Those dry lips, parted in agony. It kept me tossing in my bed until I was too tired to fight the horrible images anymore.

Despite all of this, everything seemed normal, business as usual. I woke up with the sun, to the harsh buzzing of my alarm clock, and Mary groaned from across the room, muttering about it being too early with a choice expletive. I was all too eager to welcome sunshine back into my life, but I was determined to use the extra hours before everyone else woke to do some work. I stepped into my fuzzy slippers and shrugged on a pink robe, after which I proceeded out the bedroom, down the hallway and the stairs, out the front door. I practically bounded away from the porch to rush across the street. Gabe scrambled up from where he was napping and followed me with equal exuberance. I was on a mission. I had to confirm if the dream I had last night had been prophetic.

Sure enough, as I had hoped, the body was no longer there. I glanced up toward the sky, still shadowy with the remnants of night, and I smiled.

Back to the oatmeal and the breakfast table. I just stared at the concoction while the clatter of silverware scraping on bowls filled my head obnoxiously. Our Father was exceptionally disappointed with us for being out so late, and he was disturbed by our discovery. "I just can't believe something like this would happen here," he said, "so close to home. I hope the police can identify the poor girl soon, so we can send our condolences to her family and pray for them."

No one had anything to say to this until I was too bored with my meal to stand the quiet and the organic sounds of eating. "It isn't there anymore," I announced simply. I mostly kept my eyes still on the swirls of bland cinnamon flavor in the mush, but I peeked up, sending a glance around to see what the others would say.

"Of course it isn't," Mary scoffed. "The police took it with them after we called them."

I shook my head. "No, that's wrong. The police didn't take it."

"They did, Alice!" With a sigh that seemed to carry the weight of the world, Mary glared at me. She slowed her speech, annunciating each word carefully in the suggestion that I was an imbecilic child. "The ambulance came last night to take it away. You were probably just too hysterical to notice."

I narrowed my eyes at her, though I knew no amount of glaring would convince her to take back the lie. Pushing my chair out behind me, I rose to my feet in objection. "Shut up, Mary! It wouldn't just let the cops just take it. It just opened its wi-"

"Alice! Sit down!"

There was no arguing with that voice, booming from Our Father at the other end of the table. As quickly as I had risen, I plopped back down in my seat. Silence prevailed again, to the point where even the spoons were kept as quiet as possible. Gabe started to lick at his hands, and, once again, I couldn't take it anymore. "All I'm saying," I said, my voice quiet and paced carefully as it spread across the table, "is that it just flew away. It wasn't taken by some police officer."

"Oh, Alice, honestly!" Our Father's spoon clattered into his bowl. The irises in his eyes rolled toward the ceiling, imploring for divine intervention. And then they turned hard toward Gretchen beside him. "Can't you do something about this?"

Gretchen cleared her throat, shifting uncomfortably in her chair. "Well," she spoke softly, as she always did, turning toward me with eyes and a smile that practically pleaded. "Alice, hun, let's just not talk about it right now. After breakfast, though, you can help me with the dishes, and you can tell me all about it, okay?

That was one of the amazing things about Gretchen. She could approach me with a coddling tone like that, and, instead of feeling confronted or belittled, I was happy to receive her comforting attention. It sounded like a good deal to me, since I knew that, in Gretchen, I would have a captive and open audience. I allowed myself to smile and shoveled the oatmeal into my mouth. And perhaps I might have even started to enjoy it a bit, eager to get to the bottom of the bowl.

In the kitchen, the story poured out of me with all the strength and consistency of the water from the faucet, filling the sink full of dishes. Gretchen listened intently as she splashed around and handed me newly cleansed bowls to dry. She nodded on occasion or gave a little hum of interest, and she even went so far as to acknowledge me with a word or two here and there. Every single syllable was soaked up like soapy water in the sponge of her brain.

"Gretchen," I had said, "I had a dream last night, about that body we found. It wasn't dead. It was alive, and, I swear, it asked me to help it; it even knew my name! I mean, that happened last night, and then I had a dream about it. Do you know what it told me in the dream? That it was an angel. An angel, Gretchen! It had fallen from the sky due to a terrible injustice, or a quest or message, something like that. It wouldn't tell me what it was exactly; I think I have to figure it out myself. Hm? Oh, yeah, we couldn't see its wings when we found it because they were buried under the snow. And, before you ask, I know that it flew away because it told me that in the dream, too, and there were no tracks that looked like anyone coming to get it when I checked this morning. How do I know it didn't snow over them? Don't you think I would have noticed if it snowed last night, Gretchen?"

Her questions made me laugh, questions she asked because she knew I had an answer for them, but my amusement was cut short when she stopped paying attention to me with as much focus. Her eyes had shifted toward the doorway into the kitchen from the dining room, where Our Father was standing. His gaunt face was red like fire, his neck stretched far to elevate his head. A grunt escaped his mouth first, as if making way for the words that would follow. "Alice," he said, in a stiff, strangled voice, "you had better get ready for school."

I knew to retreat from the room as quickly as possible when he used a voice like that. I shuffled out into the hallway to grab my coat, and I could hear his low voice continue. "What sort of nonsense are you allowing that girl to fill her head with now?" he asked, and I paused, coat dangling in my hand as I strained to listen in the hall. "Don't you think she's confused enough as it is? I won't have you encouraging such fanciful tales. She needs to start being more sensible. Angels! Next thing you know, she's going to be claiming she sees the Virgin Mary!"

By the time Gretchen had given a response, too quiet to make out, I realized I'd bitten my lip so hard that it started to bleed a little. I brushed my sleeve across my mouth, slinking away to find my backpack. I knew he wouldn't believe me, but that still didn't take away the aching pain of the fact that Our Father, who preached to hundreds of people every week about the glories of God, could be so reluctant to accept that divinity might grace his own daughter, as well.

***

School was hell.

"Hey, Alice!" I stopped caring who was shouting it, who was asking. "Tell us about the body again!"

"I already told you," became the typical response, "and you just laughed at me. Why should I tell you again?"

"We won't laugh this time, promise."

I sighed more times that day than I had in my entire life, forging forward with the story once again. "We found a body last night, and it was an angel. It asked for my help, but I don't know what it needs from me. I can't ask because it flew away while I was sleeping."

Uproarious laughter followed, lies exploding from their gaping, ugly mouths.

The rumors were the worst of all. The news buzzed like flies drawn to rotted fruit, feasting on everyone's elaborate ignorance of the details. It was horrible, all the untruths clashing against each other as if they were battling it out to the death. Marion Richards wasn't in school that day, so several students assumed it was her dead body we found, that she had really gotten too drunk the night before and died, but her friends ditched her in the snow because they didn't know what else to do. Most of us all denied that possibility, because the body looked nothing like Marion's would were it naked and dead, though Mary claimed otherwise. She supported the idea mostly because she wished that Marion Richards was dead. Others thought it was just some homeless girl that no one knew, one who knew too little to realize that the snow was not a safe place to sleep. Some thought it might have been Lucy, that home-schooled girl from the boarded up house at the edge of town, and that one couldn't be dispelled so easily because none of us knew what Lucy looked like. They said she must have run away, trying to escape, but was too weak from starvation to go on. Another favorite was that we all made it up. No one even bothered to believe my story, the true story. Not even Ravin and Trevor.

"You guys are my best friends! You have to believe me."

"Oh, Alice," Ravin said, turning her eyes away from me, closing them, as if she were pulling the shades down on two black-rimmed windows. The pale shame on her face was the ugliest siding I've ever seen on a house. "You know I don't believe in all that angel crap in the first place."

I turned hopefully to Trevor, who smiled awkwardly, hand dodging behind his neck. "It does seem a little far-fetched."

"Of course it's far-fetched!" I was desperate to win this case. "Do you think angels just fall out of the sky every day?"

"Well," Trevor actually stopped to think about it, or, at the very least, he pretended he did. "I suppose you're right."

"This is something special, you guys!" Pride swelled up inside me with each word. "Something amazing has happened to me. An angel asked for my help. It knew my name! It spoke to me! And you don't even feel the slightest bit happy for me…"

I couldn't stand it. I didn't want to turn away from them, but I had to, running down the hall before my tears caught up with me. I could never cry in front of Ravin; she'd hate me for it. I ducked into the bathroom, staggering over to one of the white porcelain sinks and turned the water on. I lowered my head into the lukewarm stream, rubbing it into my cheeks. My fingers gently scrubbed the water into my skin, lips parted for gasping breaths. I couldn't seem to wash away the hot tears at first, but my breathing calmed. I lifted my head, reaching for a paper towel as I sought out my own bloodshot eyes in the mirror.

What I saw instead would have made me scream if my voice hadn't gotten stuck in my throat.

There it was, the angel, behind my reflection in the mirror, its black eyes staring straight through my back. It opened its mouth, its jaw hanging slack as if about to unhinge; its pale skin looked sickly, discolored and cold. The beauty of it preserved in the snow had diminished, turning into a vulgar, decaying mess. Slowly, it lifted a hand, fingers curling toward me. Its mouth was moving like it was trying to talk, but I couldn't hear anything; not a sound came out. I could only watch the horrific attempt to communicate with my eyes practically bulging from my skull.

Then it stopped. A long moment passed with the two of us just staring at each other, until I worked up the vocal ability to speak, just a whisper, but it seemed terribly loud in the small bathroom. "What do you want from me?"

But when I turned around, there was nothing, just me, the gushing water from the faucet, and the pea soup colored tiles of the bathroom floor.

***

Gabe greeted me at the door with a cheerful yelp, bopping up and down as if caught in a popcorn maker. Feeling bad that I couldn't share his enthusiasm, I ruffled his dark blonde fur as I fell down beside him on the porch steps. My wet mittens nuzzled against my chin as I stared out across the street to the spot where we had found the body, barely visible from this point of view. I didn't want to go inside. If I did, I'd be confronted with the disbelief of Our Father, or Mary's bitter anguish over her sister being a complete and total nut job, a fucking freak, as she'd commiserated at school. If Our Father heard her talk like that, I doubt he'd despise me so much anymore, and he'd find a new daughter to be severely disappointed in, especially since Mary's cussing was hardly the worst of her.

Trevor and Ravin walked home with me, which at least helped me to stop crying, but it didn't help at all that I wasn't a single step closer to knowing what my angel wanted of me. The sight of it in the bathroom mirror, sickly and terrible, clung to my brain like a bad dream. I was distracted all through the rest of the day; I was almost booted out of math class because I kept releasing emotional outbursts at random integers. I couldn't help it, though I felt better after the walk with my friends. They left me at my stoop with Gabe, after trying to cheer me up with jokes and humorous stories. Rini and Christian both stayed out there for a while with me, too, and they even had Gretchen make me some hot chocolate when they realized that I had no intention of coming in if I could help it.

Rini pouted at me as she handed over my mug, a pout that could tear anyone's heartstrings like shredded cheese. "You're going to freeze out here, Alice."

"I can't go inside yet," I insisted. "Not until I know what it wants."

Why couldn't I piece it together? Surely there were hints. An angel wouldn't just leave you hanging without hints, but I didn't know where to find them, or even where to start looking. I started with Gabe's soulful eyes, as if they could hold the key to this riddle. He barked and started panting, clouds of stinky breath dispelling close to my nose. I had to think. If I were an angel, where would I leave my clues? Why wouldn't it let me know earlier?

Trevor's voice drifted in my head, not because he had come back, but because I just remembered something he always said to me that seemed to echo poignantly in my head at that moment. "Go back to the start," he would say, when I got overly excited and spoke too quickly and jumbled up my words. He would take me by the shoulders, lean down a little so he could look into my eyes, and calmly say, "Go back to the start."

I took off across the street before I could
even completely understand what had hit me.

***

When they brought me back into the house,
I was tired and sniffly, three inches away from the
flu, as Gretchen put it. I didn't remember falling
asleep, I didn't remember anyone finding me out
there in the snow bank, lifting me up into their
arms and carrying me home. But I do remember an
encounter with my angel, in some bleary pre-
evening gloaming, with its wings fully spread over
me in a majestic fashion. It had smiled, I
remembered that, and it was restored to its previous
beauty, as if being removed from the spot we found
it had caused its deterioration. It pointed up at the
golden light that broke through the darkness. Its
wings started to flap as it slowly ascended upwards.
I saw that it was with someone, but the light was
too bright for me to make out any details.

This had to be my clue. Changed back
from its decrepit version, it seemed to have gained
some freedom and happiness. I must be getting
close; the other person with it might have been an
additional hint. I felt dizzy, and I was shivering,
huddling up against whoever carried me across the
street and back into the house.

Our Father had given me quite an earful
when he found out that I had been outside and
fallen asleep in the same place where we'd found

the body. He started muttering all sorts of strange prayers and hymns, gripping my forehead and raving about the influence of the Devil. When I tried to explain that it was an angel, not a devil, I was slapped, hard, and he continued. He eventually exhausted himself, leaving to pray on his own, which left me to sort things out by myself. I thought of crawling back outside but, feeling the effects of the cold run down from my nose again, I decided to take refuge in a warmer, even more familiar place.

Placidly, fighting back a sniffle, I made my way to the small sitting room that faced the setting sun, the place that earned itself the title of The Forbidden Room when my siblings and I were younger. It was a serene place, one that Our Father hadn't touched since Mom died. Gretchen would clean the dust away from the antique table, the towering bookshelves, the porcelain dolls placed on high shelves, but she would never move anything, only keep it clean out of respect. I shuffled in, my bare toes rolling joyfully in the thick, plush carpet. I made a slow circle around the outside of the room, my fingers drifting lightly over everything, pausing sometimes to savor certain memories. A picture of the entire family, back when it was complete, with the sisters I never saw anymore huddling around Our Father, Christian and Rini settled in Mom's lap, still too young to stand on their own, Mary and me actually hugging each other. And there were all the books filled with fairy tales, wonderfully old books I couldn't bear to open anymore, ones she'd read from for at least half an hour a night, even though we were only supposed to have one story before bed. The precious dolls she had made to resemble some fantastical image of her children were settled comfortably on the small loveseat.

I stopped, though, as I always did, when I reached her prayer book. It was in a special spot on the table beside her large leather armchair, and Our Father had left it eternally opened to a passage on Matthew 18:10, a shrine to her passing. Every time I see it, I have to close my eyes tightly to help with the fact that I miss her so much it hurts.

***

When Gretchen passed by the room several hours later, she found me huddled in the large leather armchair. Just sitting there. I was too tired for anything else, though I still let the tears roll ceaselessly down my cheeks. She smiled softly at me, and I moved my head, slowly moving the scrap of paper in my hand to my side so she wouldn't see it. She didn't say anything; she didn't have to. She just moved over for a moment and rested her hand on my head, gently running her palm along my hair. She disappeared into the darkened house as subtly as she arrived, and my eyes intently stared into the darkness before I slipped off the chair and pushed the old photograph of Mom into my pocket and quietly left the room.

***

After all that crying, draining everything inside of me, I thought I'd be able to sleep, but I was wrong. Something was there, lingering at the back of my mind, and it wouldn't let go. It was the angel, it had to be, reminding me that my work wasn't entirely done, not yet. Honestly, though, I was finished. I had given up and wanted nothing more to do with the angel, but the angel wouldn't give me peace. I was in it for good.

I resisted as long as I could, but then I found myself muttering into my pillow and getting up. "Fine," I said petulantly, "you win."

I padded out onto the cold hardwood floors of the hallways with bare feet while the rest of the house was still fast asleep. I tried to move as quickly as I could, hopping from rug to rug on a nerve-wrecking quest not to wake anyone up. As I approached Our Father's room, I could hear his snores, low and drawn out. Even in his sleep, he prayed, sending out the earnest wishes of pious chainsaws. I slipped into his bedroom, halting at every small shift in his blankets, edging along until I had reached the door to his study.

My caution in closing the door couldn't prevent the grating groan of its hinges, which I thought would certainly bring Our Father out of his slumber and me one step closer into hell, but he slept blissfully on. I breathed for the first time in what felt like five minutes. The dangerous trek in the dark to his desk was made successfully without any bashed toes or shins, and I cringed at the click made by the lamp on his desk as I turned it on. I winced at the bright light.

Recovering, I set about searching the books on Our Father's shelves, scanning the leather-bound volumes for one particular manuscript. Bibles of various translations and editions passed my eyes, books of saints and religious musings, all worn and well-read, until I finally found it. The Encyclopedia of Angels. Smiling a bit, I tucked my finger into the top of its spine and slid it from its companions.

Trusting faith to guide me, I split the covers to a random page. I figured that if I were going to discover anything about my angel, it would be here. I tried to focus on the small print on the yellowed pages, but what I discovered instead was a small, creased photograph. I blinked, my mouth going dry. It was old, and with a quick repositioning of it, I saw a startling image of my mother, younger than I had ever seen her, and absolutely radiant. Her skin was paled by the picture's age, but her smile was still bright and full of life. Red hair spilled in loose curls about her shoulders, feathery wings peeking out from behind her back. A small yellow halo was suspended above her head by two thin wires. Drawing in a deep breath, I gingerly flipped the picture over to the simple words scribed onto the back.

Halloween 1966. Matthew, Sweetheart, I'll Always Be Your Angel.

I had to sit down. Suddenly, it all made sense, and I was stunned that I didn't realize it earlier, but that face looking at me from the picture was the same face I saw earlier that evening with the angel. It had been looking down on me, smiling, watching over me.

***

The next morning, there was an article in the newspaper detailing the specifics of the concluded police report. It announced to the public that the body found earlier that week by the children of a local pastor belonged to a young woman named Rachel Morris, a student at the university. Apparently, under the influence of some highly potent drug, she staggered from a friend's party, gotten too hot for her clothing, then fell asleep in an unfamiliar and unusual bed. There was a picture of her accompanying the article, and I do have to admit, she bears an uncanny resemblance to my angel. In a way, I don't blame the officials for releasing the story. It would be much easier for everyone to swallow the idea of collegiate debauchery than to choke down a tale about angels helping young women find peace in their hearts.

It's better they went with the other story; the world might not quite be ready for a truth like that.

Just Right

At the sound of the buzzer, the large metal doors unlatched and slid open; patients dressed in their pale pink uniforms shuffled through, single file, into the mess hall. Wedged in her usual orderly spot, Gohalla Daffodil Lox, known simply as Goh, kept her head hung low, a spiral of blonde hair escaping, as always, to dangle in her eyes. She wanted to brush it back, but doing so would be difficult with her hands folded discretely in front of her, not by choice, but by the heavy shackles keeping her bound to the line of other patients. All in a row, with steady, sometimes dragging steps, they approached the tables, their line becoming parallel with the long benches flanking the tables. Uniformly, they all turned to the table at the same time and waited for the next buzzer, which prompted them to sit; each one of them kept their wrists held up over the table and dropped them down together with a clatter of the chain in between them. A third buzzer sounded, and the metal circles around their wrists broke away, opening like cracked eggs and dissolving neatly into the metal surface of the table. They'd be back, at the end of the meal, but, for now, their wrists and hands were free to maneuver their flatware and help them eat their food. The sensors were still active, though, ready to give them a smart little zap if any of them decided to try any funny business.

Even with her hands free, Goh didn't feel comfortable brushing the hair from her eyes; the sensor might misinterpret her actions and shock her. So she just hunched her shoulders forward as she waited, puffing out a stream of air in the hopes that it would blow the curl away. It lifted for a second, but then settled right back where it had been, and Goh sighed, giving up.

"I need a haircut," she murmured, her eyes crossing as she accusingly eyed the rogue tendril.

"Be careful what you wish for," said Murr from across the table, with a sing-song voice and a bitter smile. "You'll wind up with no hair at all, just like Punzel!" She sent her silently laughing grin toward the empty spot where the young woman named Punzel used to sit. She wasn't there today, which wasn't uncommon. They were more likely to see her seat vacant than they were to see her sitting in it.

"Hair today, gone tomorrow," Murr added blithely.

Goh wrinkled her nose at Murr, ready to meet her distasteful comments with a sharp one of her own, but Snow sitting beside her managed to interject. "Oh, but it's got to be an improvement," she said, sweetly injecting her perfect timing into the situation to keep it from going sour. "A face like that, hiding under all that hair, and we'd have never known it!"

"And it'll stay hidden, the way she's gotten herself shoved into solitary again," Goh pointed out. She didn't agree with Murr's obvious pleasure from poor Punzel's pain, but she found Snow's saccharine sympathy just as irritating. "What did she even do to deserve something like that? I'm pretty sure that classifies as cruel and unusual—"

The final buzzer until the end of the meal session cut her off, resounding loudly over the voices rising up from the lines. All conversation cut as eyes shifted to the surface of the table, which slid away in sections, revealing a little platform that lifted to bring their meal up to them. A collective groan rippled through the hall as every one of them peered down into the steaming bowls set before them, in the middle of plastic cutlery, napkins, and a metal cup filled with protein water.

"Porridge again!" Murr let out a near-wail of despair, her tongue rolling out as she made strangling, choking sounds. Still, she seized her spoon and started swirling around the colorless mush inside her bowl. She scooped some out, tilting the utensil sideways and making faces at the slow gruel as it glopped back into her bowl. The second spoonful, though, found its way into her mouth.

Goh took her time, frowning down at the mush before patting it with the back of her spoon. It made a slight squishing sound, and pieces of the meal clung to the spoon like glue, but at least it would sit better in her stomach than when they made it so runny it was practically a rehydrated oat soup.

"They can never get it just right, can they?" she murmured with disappointment. "Too hot, too cold. Too runny, too thick. It's porridge; how hard can it be?"

"It's still better than nothing at all," Snow said, her big blue eyes shifting toward the gates where the guards stood watching, hoping the comments weren't overheard and misinterpreted. Goh followed Snow's eyes, but she knew that the guards were just as disenchanted with this place as the women they were guarding. She could probably curse out all of their mothers and the entire establishment as a whole, and they wouldn't even blink an eye, so long as she was sitting down, nice and put, while she did it. That was no skin off Goh's nose, though. In fact, she planned to use it to her advantage.

Goh looked over the faces around the table, carefully taking into consideration who was sitting near. She took in a spoonful of the horrible, tasteless glop they tried to pass as food, then calmly announced to her compatriots, "I think I'm doing it tonight."

The women around her stopped eating. Murr almost dropped her spoon right into her porridge. Quickly, they tried to mask their shocked expressions before they were noticed, drawing even more attention to their sudden halt in conversation and eating.

"You can't be serious!" Cindy hissed, leaning forward over the table with her fierce eyes fixed on Goh like a cold steel vice, covered in a sheen of fear. "I thought that was all just some sick joke!"

"Do you think you can pull it off?" Lucy blinked her wide, owlish eyes at Goh with shock and admiration.

"No one can pull it off," said Murr, shaking her head, swirling her porridge. "That includes you, Goh."

"No one's pulled it off because no one has been smart enough to figure out how to do it," Goh insisted. "Half the girls in this joint are idiots, and the other half are legitimately insane. I've spent a lot of my life breaking into places, you guys. How much more difficult can it be to break out?"

But Snow shook her head, glancing at the guards again to make sure they hadn't drawn any attention. For good measure, she scooped up some porridge and swallowed a bite before continuing, knowing that it could spark suspicion if the sensors realized they were spending more time moving their jaws for talking rather than masticating. "A lot more difficult," she said. "You know I'd want nothing more than for someone to get out of here, but this place was designed to keep people in, Goh. Forget all the guards; what happens when you get out of this place?"

"It's true." Stern and quiet Gretel stared at Goh in a way that made Goh straighten her shoulders in defiance, even though it was impossible to discern exactly what Gretel meant with her steady, unnerving expression. "There's something wrong with the woods out there. They designed it so that no one can get out, ever. It's like a labyrinth that just keeps circling back on itself, the same thing, over and over and over. You could get out of this building, Goh, but you'll never get out of the woods."

"That's bullshit," said Goh. "How do the guards get home, then? Or the doctors, or people who have visitors? They don't have trouble coming in and out. They just started that rumor to scare us, to keep us in place! It's all a big fat lie."

But the way Gretel kept staring at her made Goh shift uncomfortably on her bench. She braced herself for another bite of the terrible porridge, forcing it down in a hard swallow before continuing. "Besides, even if it is true and I get caught, what's the worst they could do?"

The silence settled over the table, like the heavy porridge settled in their stomachs, and Goh realized she shouldn't have asked. Each and every one of them, she knew, could come up with some terrible answer to that question and some far worse as well. She bit her lip for a moment, feeling nausea rise up into her throat, and she forced it down with a bit of a cough. "Forget I asked," she muttered, lowering her head, golden curls tumbling forward, and she decided perhaps she wouldn't bring her plans up anymore. She was confident it would work, even if they weren't, so she would have to continue without them.

***

Dr. Wilhelm Grimm, Ph.D., lifted his eyes, peering over the folder in his hands, at the young woman in the large leather arm chair. Goh shifted uncomfortably under his gaze. She wanted to stare back at him in defiance, but she couldn't help lowering her eyes, fiddling with her fingers in her lap. There was something about the doctor's eyes that made her feel particularly nervous, almost ill, the pale, cool gaze sizing her up, judging her, analyzing her. He sighed, a disappointed sound, looking back down at the folder one more time before lightly closing it. He tossed it carefully on the desk and leaned forward, lacing his fingers together and setting them on top of the file. His little round glasses were slipping down his slender nose, but he did not bother pushing them back up. His beady gaze penetrated through Goh from behind the gold frames.

"Miss Lox," he said, in that obnoxiously pretentious formality he insisted on holding with all his patients, "the reports from your supervisors have been very positive. I must commend you on your very positive progress. Only a handful of items have gone missing, later to be found in your possession, and Nurse Mal tells me you've ceased all attempts to try to get into the nurses' station on your floor, that you've even stopped going into your fellow patients' rooms. This is exceptionally pleasing to me, Miss Lox."

Never knowing how to respond to works of praise, especially knowing they were probably rife with dangerous implications, Goh merely mumbled something unintelligible, only glancing up briefly toward the doctor, past the curl of hair in her eye.

"I'm sorry, Miss Lox," Grimm said, shaking his head. "I did not catch that. Your sticky fingers may be curing quickly, but your annunciation is rather atrocious."

"I said," Goh choked back her irritation, "thank you, sir."

A smile instantly blossomed on Grimm's face, but it was not an attractive expression. It was predatory, the smile of a dog about to bite. "No need to thank me, Miss Lox. The work is all yours! What, pray tell, do you suppose has inspired this positive transformation? Have you had any breakthroughs in your psyche?"

Goh had to push down her groan before it bubbled out of her. Breakthroughs in her psyche. Every week, she was dragged out of her cell and into this office, and she was expected to speak with the doctor about all of her problems and issues, as if the activity of talking could cure her of all the things they'd deemed wrong with her. Complete bullshit. It wasn't that she'd stopped stealing; she was just getting better at not getting caught. And, besides, if she had ceased, it was merely because she wanted to suspend any extra attention afforded to her. The more they paid attention to her, the harder it would be to escape, so she had to ensure that she was regarded as mostly harmless, improving slowly thanks to their bullshit program.

She still had to think of something to tell him to satiate his perverse inquisitiveness. "Well," she said, slowly, carefully, trying to think quickly on her feet, "I suppose losing Punzel had an awful lot to do with that, Doctor. It was such a wake-up call. If I don't change my ways, then there's a good chance I might end up in solitary, too, right?"

Peering over, trying to look innocent and frightened, Goh was pleased to see that her question had the right response. In his clean tweed suit, Grimm bristled, stiffening and adjusting his tie as if the room had suddenly grown hot and uncomfortable. "Well, as you know," he said, "Miss Punzel is a very special case, Miss Lox. But I suppose if her mistakes can help you other girls from making the same ones in the future, then perhaps some good has come from her unfortunate predicament."

Goh nodded gravely, feeling like a trained animal as she did so, but she reminded herself that, so long as she didn't start to believe what she told them herself, she would get out of this alive.

***

It rained that night, a long, windy, heavy rain that pounded on the windows of the common living area where some of the patients were allowed to sit and socialize, if they were good, if they weren't causing any trouble, if whichever nurse was on duty could manage keeping a handful of them in line. Since she'd been doing so well, as Dr. Grimm had said, Goh was allowed to be there, though she was considering going back to her cell anyway. The rain had the television set on the fritz, good for little more than static and blurbled speech, and the flickering light had set some of the patients off, so they were mostly sitting in the dark, save for a few lamps, with little to do but count the seconds between flashes of lightning.

The living area sat at the end of the hall lined with doors to their cells. While those harsh cubicles had the stark and barren effect of a prison, there was an odd sort of hominess about the sitting room. Three large windows looked out over the forest surrounding the facility, flanked with heavy curtains. There was carpet here, too, plush rugs that were soft and easy on the knees, since so many of them were wont to throw sudden fits. The couches and chairs were also all very soft, lest anyone bash their head on a corner or try to harm themselves. There were a few tables with rounded edges, usually holding puzzles or board games. A battered shelf held a few worn and tattered books, and there was also a stack of fashion and gossip magazines, read far more than any of the books. Mostly, though, the girls just went there for a splash of color and home, to get out of their cells and pretend for a moment that they weren't as messed up as they were, that their situations weren't so grim.

Eventually, the quiet got to someone and the girls would talk, a tentative voice rising up to encourage the others. This time, the little feathery voice came from the waif named Lucy. She stood by the window, her long slender fingers stroking the glass almost tenderly. "Just think," she mused. "All these spring showers will bring out all the pretty flowers, and the geese will come back from the south. Won't that be lovely?"

"Real lovely." Cindy snorted from a corner of the room. She was on her knees, with a brush, obsessively going through the motions of cleaning the floor even though she had no soap or water. She swept a strand of her ashen hair away from her face. "All that goose shit to clean off the sidewalks!"

"They won't shit on the sidewalks," Lucy said, petulantly glaring at Cindy's prone figure. "They'll stay near the pond and in the woods, where they belong."

"Where they hide all their golden eggs," another girl put in; Goh couldn't tell who, but it made the others laugh. It was a nervous laugh, though, uncertain and a little afraid; from what they'd heard about the golden eggs, they were hardly a laughing matter. But Goh figured that anyone stupid enough to take a golden egg after hearing all the stories about them deserved whatever punishment came their way. Her mind was slipping toward something else, though, as she watched the rain cascade down the window panes, thinking of the freedom outside these walls.

"Do you really think it's true?" Goh eventually asked, after a glance over her shoulder to see what the nurse was up to. She was making notes on a clipboard, but, other than that, seemed to be paying little attention to the patients since they were being so quiet and well-behaved. "That there's something out there that makes it difficult to get out of the forest? It just doesn't make any sense."

Snow gave her a little smile. "You won't know unless you try, right?"

The twinkle in the other girl's eyes made Goh snort. "Right," she said. "Too bad it's fucking raining right now, or I'd be out of here quicker than you can say Big Bad Wolf. I think it's coming, though, Snow. Soon. And you're right. I guess I'll find out."

"Good luck," said Snow, and Goh knew she meant it. The other woman's confidence and encouragement seemed to have blossomed over the last few days. It was true; she really wanted to see someone finally get out of this place.

"Just remember to leave bread crumbs," said Gretel, looking up from her crayon drawings with a plaintive look that sent Goh's spine on edge. Gretel stared at her for a moment before dropping her head and returning to her artwork, but it stuck with Goh for a long time, even after she'd excused herself and went to find the guard to escort her back to her cell. She realized she preferred the coldness of her cell to the coldness of Gretel's haunted gaze.

***

The most challenging part of Goh's ultimate plan for escape was getting out of the building in the first place. She was sure she wouldn't have any issues with things once she was outside the walls, but breaking free of a high-security prison was a step or two up from sneaking out of her bed at night when she was in the state homes. She had a bad habit of twisting her long golden curls around her finger and sucking at the ends when she thought hard about something, staring wide eyed at a spot on the wall. When she realized she had been doing it as she contemplated the technicalities of her escape, she stopped, wondering if anyone had noticed. So many of the patients were so far gone that everyone probably just assumed she was slipping down the slope to insanity with them.

Over her dead body. Some of them, like Snow and Cindy, might be content where they were, but Goh would waste away if she didn't get out. Nothing fit right here. The food was terrible, the furniture uncomfortable, and she was certain she was slowly, slowly going mad with what they were doing to them all in this glorified institution and correctional facility.

In the corner of her cell, perched on the edge of her bed, Goh sucked on her hair and thought. The best time would be during free time in the living area. Perhaps someone could create a distraction. Gretel could have a fit or maybe Cindy could cause an outburst, but the problem that was that Goh wasn't sure she could trust either of them. They'd have to be bought, but with what? Murr was just a bitch, and Lucy was too flighty. The only one she completely trusted was Snow, and Snow could never pull it off.

The sucking on the end of her hair became chewing. There had to be a solution. There had to be an answer somewhere.

The opportunity arose out of nowhere, unexpected, unplanned, and completely perfect. It was another quiet afternoon in the living room. The sun outside appeared impossibly bright, the sort of spring day that only existed in memories of more innocent times. Through the large windows, Goh could see the forest stretching out, and she could trace the path she would take to her freedom, if only she could just get out.

That was when it happened. As sudden as a flash of lightning, a scream emerged from the middle of the room, where Gretel had been sitting on the floor with her crayons again. "No!" she shouted, interspersed with a terrible whimper as she writhed where she sat. All heads turned toward her; someone let out a laugh, but there was little humor in the terrified convulsions taking over the young woman's round, childish face. "Hot," she panted, curling a hand into her clothes and pulling, ineffectually trying to yank the pink uniform away from her body. "Too hot. Oh, God, I'm burning, burning, it's too hot!"

Nearly everyone stood stock still, staring wide-eyed as Gretel's body contorted and twisted, falling onto the floor, squirming to get out of the clothing that seemed to be burning her. It had been so long since anyone had had an episode like this that even the nurse forgot what to do for a moment. Eventually, she shouted, "Everyone stand back!" She jogged her hand down on the counter before reaching for a medical kit and fled from inside her little booth into the living room. The door clattered behind her, and Goh realized that this was it. Her eyes fell toward Gretel for a moment, her face red and her shouts mingling with sudden sobs about burning, about flames, hellfire and consumption and pain, and a pang of regret swelled up in Goh's stomach. She and Gretel were not friends, but there was something about using someone else's pain for her own gain that made her feel terrible. She realized, though, that this was the only chance she'd get. She only had a few minutes before the doctors would receive the signal from the emergency button pushed by nurse, and they'd come thundering in.

With the nurse at Gretel's side, there was no one to notice Goh slipping by, towards the door, to crouch by the entrance and wait for the doctors to come in. She had no tools to pick the lock, but if she could keep herself hidden when they came in, she could slip through before the door closed behind them, unnoticed and moving down the hall and onward to her freedom.

Well, almost unnoticed. As she crouched at the ready, Goh glanced back to the living room and saw Snow's big blue eyes staring at her, mystified. Goh lifted a finger to her lips, prompting Snow to silence about what she was about to witness. Snow nodded in silent agreement. She could hear them coming, their feet clattering on the linoleum floor. It was almost time.

***

Her first breath of fresh air almost hurt.

It wasn't as though Goh had been deprived of the outside world. There were outings and walks and grounds work to be done, but this was the first time in a long time that there was a thread of freedom laced into the oxygen, and that made all the difference. It was still sunny and warm, a storybook afternoon, and Goh figured that would work to her advantage. In the darkness, beneath the cover of storms, one would expect people to try to escape. She doubted people would expect anyone to try to slip out in broad daylight. The pleasant weather would make the guards lazy and distracted, their minds on things other than the dark and dreary patients they were supposed to be watching.

She would just have to be careful, slipping between buildings and trees until she was at the gate. Goh's eyes drifted upwards, scaling the tall fence toward the spirals of barbed wire decorating the top like icing on a terrible cake. She swallowed the lump in her throat. Everyone knew it was impossible to climb those fences. Even if you were good enough and found a way to slip past the barbed wire without being ripped to shreds, you would be an obvious target for the watchtower guards and their deadly precision with a sniper rifle. Not too long ago, a young man from the men's ward had made the attempt; they said the guards let him scale up to the very top before shooting him. They didn't shoot him dead, though, avoiding anything vital by nicking his shoulder, so that he would lose his grip on the fence. It wasn't the shot that killed him, but rather the impact with the ground once he got there.

That was where the north corner came in. Paranoid people like Alice suggested that the hole in the north corner gate was left there intentionally; that, long ago, someone had dug it out and slipped through, but since the forest beyond the facility was a much more gruesome and effective barrier against escape, they left it there, so that anyone who would be so bold as to use it would find themselves in a predicament far worse than anything they could experience inside the facility's gates. Part of Goh easily believed it. Hidden behind a bush and surprisingly easy to miss if you weren't looking directly at it, the Hole in the Gate was one of those details that even the administration would likely discover eventually. They were thorough and paid an incredible amount of attention to detail, but, sure enough, as Goh made her way across the lawn, the hole was still there, unmended and waiting for her. She breathed a sigh of relief; she half expected it to be one of the many false myths surrounding this place.

A faint thought drifted unbidden into her consciousness. If the Hole in the Fence was not a myth, then what if perhaps the story about the forest's impossibility was also true? She shook her head; she wasn't going to allow herself to think like that. She was going to get out of this place.

She had to.

Behind the bush, Goh lowered herself to her hands and knees, peering through the Hole in the Fence, considering the scoop of earth that would allow for a body to pass through, but just barely. It looked like the sort of thing a dog might dig. Big Bad Wolf, she thought, though she remembered Alice insisting it was a rabbit. It must have been one massive bunny if that was true, even though she realized, as her finger brushed against the sharp points of the torn metal, it was still a tight squeeze for her. She closed her eyes, pressed herself down close to the earth, and tried to imagine herself as small as she possibly could while crawling forward.

The sharp ends dug into her shirt; she felt it tangle in her golden curls. It raked harshly against her skin, and she almost called out in surprise and pain, but she froze where she was, half in, half out, when she realized that someone was passing by. One of the guards, no doubt, making a round. Goh froze, still as she could. She closed her eyes, waiting for the guard to pass. She hoped that she was concealed by the bush, that her feet weren't poking out, that her golden hair might not catch his eye through the green of the bush. She closed her eyes tightly and tried not to move, waiting for him to pass.

The wait stretched on forever; Goh couldn't be certain if it was time that was slowing, or merely the guard himself, suddenly moving as though at a snail's pace. It was excruciating. Could she hold her breath that long? Could she hold still? What if she did something as uncontrollable as twitching her leg, sending the bush shuddering with rustling leaves, and that would be all it took to catch the guard's notice and she'd be done for it? She'd be thrown into solitary for her attempt, or, worse, she'd be subject to more tests, more brain probing and blood drawing, more thresholds of pain to see what might be wrung out of her in the throes of torture. Biting down on her lip, Goh made herself stop thinking about these things, lest she inspire a shudder through her entire body, and then her imagination would become reality.

Once she escaped from this place, all of that would be history. She would focus on that. There would probably be a time, until she managed to get as far away from the facility as she could, where she'd have to watch her back, when they would likely be looking for her and intending to bring her back into custody, but, after a while, they would stop caring, so long as she laid low. No more breaking into government buildings...or anywhere, really, though it had been the Hall of Records that had gotten her in this predicament. She couldn't believe she'd ever through it had been a good idea in the first place. But she also believed that information should be free. They had no right to hold that back from her. She deserved to know the truth about her parents' death.

Goh closed her eyes and scolded herself. If she kept thinking, she was going to get upset, and if she got upset, then she would flub this attempt. She needed to just focus on the guard and his placid steps, and on getting the most out of her time once her window of opportunity had opened again.

After the guard passed, she waited at least another two minutes...or was it more? It felt like more, dragging by with each second filled with a sweating distress...before she started scooting herself forward again. The sharp ends of the fence dug into her sides; it took everything she had not to cry out in pain, but once her hips had cleared, it was smooth sailing and she felt the freedom open up around her as she scrambled to her feet.

She should have started running right then, the moment she'd been free of the fence, but a part of her couldn't help turning around. She wanted one last look at that tall stone building, the place that had been her prison for so long now. On this side of the fence, it looked grey and bleak, the colors of the greenery of the grounds faded into a sad, dilapidated place where dreams went to die. The only color that really stood out was hooked around the outside of the fence, a tendril of her golden hair, caught up, torn out, and left like a banner. Goh's hand traveled to the side of her head, as if she could feel the spot where the hair had gotten caught, and she felt a great urge to snatch up the hair and take it with her. Leaving it there was like leaving a little bit of herself behind. But, as her eyes passed up toward one of the windows looking out over the forest, she decided to keep it there, after all. For the next girl that managed to escape. And for the fact that there would always be a piece of her left behind, inside those walls, and it could never be recovered.

Goh turned and started running, into the dark shadows of the thick green forest that circled the hospital, underneath the canopy that would cover her until she finally reached the world beyond. The ground felt uneven under her feet; rocks threatened her balance as she ran and branches whipped at her face, but she paid them no heed. She just pushed through the foliage, determined and dedicated to make it through, to make it as far as she could go before they realized that she was gone and sent someone after her. It would be insanely difficult for them to find her, though, she realized. The trees were getting thicker by the second, the brush surrounding her, almost protecting her, and she knew if she stood still, even in her pink uniform with her golden hair, she might be able to hide in the thick foliage of the healthy forest.

This was it, she realized, with a rush so exalting that it swept her breath away. She was free. She could taste it, smell it, touch it with her hand against the cool, rough bark of a tree. She let out a laugh, and it echoed against the canopy and sent a small flock of birds flapping toward the sky. She felt the vigor of life racing through her, she felt as though color was returning to her cheeks. She looked behind her and she could no longer see the facility, though she could see the gate, and she could still see that dancing thread of golden hair.

"This is it," she said, to the flowers, the bushes, the trees, to the blue sky that she could see peeking through the thick layer of leaves over her head. "I made it!"

***

The novelty of Goh's newfound freedom was one that wore off quickly, especially after she started to suspect there was some validity in the musings that one might escape from the physical prison itself, only to enter into a new prison entirely. The warm sunshine of the afternoon was fading, the air cooling as the inevitable evening set in. To add to the predicament, Goh felt as though she hadn't made any progress whatsoever. She could no longer see the building; the fence had disappeared behind walls of trees, but she felt as though she were passing through the same scenes over and over again. She tried to tell herself she was just letting her imagination get away with her. That rock only seemed familiar because rocks weren't very different. That outcropping only seemed to be the same one she'd noticed ten minutes ago because there were so many of them around. If no one had ever said anything about this forest being inescapable, she'd have never have thought such things. It was all in her head.

She thought of Gretel and her bread crumbs. Her stomach rumbled, reminding her of another problem that demanded her attention, but she tried to ignore it. There was a good chance she could find some berries or nuts, and that would help with her growing hunger, though it seemed a very unsatisfactory solution. Goh bit her lip, looking around her at the scenery. She looked down, to the hem of her uniform, and her fingers took a hold of it. She pulled and tugged but the cloth didn't give away until she took her teeth to it, and the ripping sound seemed to echo through the trees. Goh paused, looking up, petrified that the sound might alert anything that might be lurking in the thickening shadows, but there was nothing.

Goh finished tearing off the strip of clothing and tied it carefully around the branch of a tree. She gave it a tug to ensure it stayed put, and then started out again in another direction, ready to mark another spot within view so she could follow her path a little better.

Her eyes searched for spots of color, for signs of food or something that could work as a shelter. She hadn't expected this to take so long; by night, she had expected to be through the woods and on the road, but now she was concerned. Big Bad Wolf was another myth, just like the never-ending forest, but she knew that it was inspired by the fact that there were plenty of wolves in these woods. One could hear them howling their haunting songs in the middle of the night, sending shivers up your spine. Goh hadn't heard any yet today, but she definitely did not want to.

Besides, she had found the golden eggs. She knew better than to touch them, but the sight of them gleaming menacingly from the underbrush made her shiver. If the golden eggs existed, and she was lost in the forest with no sign of getting out, what other rumors were true? She didn't want to think about it. She couldn't think about it, not if she wanted to get out of here.

She pushed aside some branches and stepped out into a small clearing of grass, and immediately let out a gasp of frustration. Wrapped around the branch of one of the trees was a small banner of pink cloth, stark against the darkness of the bark. Goh ran up to it, wondering if it was some other swatch; it couldn't possibly be hers! But it was as clean and bright as her own clothing now; the edge was still damp with the saliva from her mouth. Overwrought with exhaustion and irritation, Goh let out a cry and sunk down to the forest floor with defeat.

She should have never left. She should have stayed where she was, continued to pretend to be well-behaved and reformed, and, eventually, they'd have just let her out on good behavior. Instead, she had to be bold and brash and try to escape; she had to ignore the warnings around her and forge ahead. She had to be different and decided she could escape, that she could succeed where no one else could.

Despite her best efforts to hold it back, Goh dropped down to the ground and began to cry. She had cried only a few times in her life, and she could barely remember the last time, except for a haze of unclear details. A dark alley in the city somewhere, and her parents dead, her small fist clinging to the blood-soaked shirt of her father's suit.

Goh hated crying. Crying was a waste of energy, a waste of emotion, a waste of time. After letting it out, though, she pulled herself up, forcing herself to stop, feeling minutely better. She sniffed, running the back of her hand under her nose to wipe away the warm, watery snot. She turned her bleary eyes toward the sky. Clearing her throat, she sniffed again.

This time, she sniffed to smell. She thought she had caught the faint scent of something in the air, but she was sure it had to be her imagination.

No, it was undeniable. She smelled smoke, faint but heavy, not of a simple fire, but of a hearth, with the suggestion of home and comfort in it. Where would there be a fire out here in the middle of nowhere? She thought perhaps it might be the guards sent to find her, making camp, but that seemed impossible. There was a homey scent to it, tinged with sweetness and cinnamon, like someone baking something fresh and wonderful.

Goh scrambled to her feet, brushed the leaves off her knees, and started in the direction of the curious scent. She approached with caution and confusion, no less astounded when she finally found the source.

It was only a small walk from where she had been, which was just astonishing as the fact that it had been there at all, since Goh was certain she'd been drifting through the same scenes again and again, and it would be hard not notice a house, much less one with a tall red chimney gently puffing out smoke. It wasn't a big house, but it stood two stories tall, with cheerful flower boxes against its windows and a welcoming red door. It sat in a small clearing, with a sprawling vegetable patch at one side, and Goh's stomach instantly growled as she looked over the tufts of root vegetables and the beans climbing up plastic poles, the occasional suggestion of a red berry hidden under low leaves.

She moved forward with slow, careful steps, glancing over her shoulder as if to ensure that she was out of the range of the facility. Exactly how far had she gone? Perhaps she had finally gotten through the grounds, and she stood now in new territory, free territory, where perhaps normal people lived in their quiet little cabins in the wood. Goh drew in a deep breath, filling her senses with the scent and promise of cinnamon, and she sighed out gratefully.

She crept with quiet feet toward the door. Whoever these people were, she suspected they had to be home, the way their fireplace was going, but everything was so still, so quiet. She tried to move as stealthily as possible across the lawn, closer to the building itself, so she could get a better look and listen for the sounds of life inside. Voices. A television set. Creaking floorboards or movement in a kitchen. But she heard nothing, except the sound of birds twittering in the trees and a squirrel dashing across a branch.

Satisfied in her assessment that the occupants were actually out, Goh dropped to her knees in front of the garden and dug her hands under the leaves to get at the berries. She spared no time in plucking off their stems and popping them into her mouth, reaching for more before the first ones were even swallowed. The cool juice flowed down her chin; she idly wiped it away with the back of her hand, snapping off a few beans, pulling out a few carrots. The more she ate, though, the more she realized that the carrots were mealy and unsatisfactory, the berries a little bitter, and the beans tough and starchy.

With a little bit of food in her stomach, Goh felt more content and her perspective was changing. This was good; she was away from the facility, she now had some food, she was on the right track. She glanced again toward the house, which seemed inviting, tempting her, and her attention turned to her clothes. The bright pink was a clear give-away that she was a patient, and there was a good chance that there were some clothes inside the house that she could spirit away to gain her some more purchase. Her fingers were itching, too, to try that lock, to see just what she could get away with.

Goh had enough sense to hesitate. This was exactly what had gotten her in this predicament in the first place, that driving need to go where she wasn't supposed to, to take what wasn't hers, as if that would bring back everything that had been taken from her. If she didn't safeguard herself, though, get some new clothes, some food for the road, she'd be screwed

After this, she could try to live a different life, but there were a few more hills to climb before the terrain evened out, a storm to brave before there was smoother sailing.

She got up from the garden, brushed the dirt off of her uniform and her hands, and walked around to the back of the house. Somehow, breaking into a home through the front door seemed a violation of how things were done, but there was no back door. The windows, with their flower boxes, would be difficult to get to, so she circled around to the front again. Somewhere, in the back of her head, Goh felt like something was wrong, and she realized there was no access to a road. Even get-away cabins usually had a two-track for a vehicle, didn't they, for when their owners drove in from the city for the weekend? But there was nothing like that here, no sign of a vehicle anywhere. Goh shook her head, wondering if her thoughts were straying because she was getting drained after the adrenaline of her escape, and she came around to the front door.

There was a tiny stoop in front of the cheerful door; she carefully stepped up to peek in through the window. It looked into a cozy little living room, big plushy chairs and thick rugs, the walls wooden with hanging pictures. Sure enough, a cheerful little fire danced in a stone fireplace. Though a pleasant evening was settling in, Goh shivered, realizing how cozy that fire must be.

When she tried the door, it was unlocked.

If the door was unlocked, was it really breaking and entering? Trespassing, perhaps, but anyone who left doors unlocked was asking for that sort of thing to happen. She could argue, too, that the owners of this house lived out in the middle of nowhere; they probably didn't expect a lot of visitors. On the other hand, the closest thing nearby was one of the state's largest facilities for the criminally insane. That concluded it. They were idiots for leaving their home so readily accessible, and she was barely going to take anything, anyway.

"Ugh." Goh realized what she was doing and made a face at the door. Her incarceration had warped her mind, making her analyze everything she did, exploring her actions and justifying them. She never doubted herself like this before. She brushed away all the pyscho bullshit reasoning and waltzed confidently into the building, refusing to be hindered by the morality imposed on her from within those walls.

Just as she imagined from her peek through the window, the main room was warm and comfortable, picturesque in its coziness. There was a plush, decorative rug spread out over the dark hardwood floor; three armchairs sat gathered around the fireplace, and the walls were lined with shelves of books. There was a table with a lamp in it, a ball of yarn and a pair of knitting needles. There was something that looked like a scarf in the process of being finished, and there was a wooden toy train, its caboose upended on its side, on the floor. A newspaper folded on another side table. The fire crackled cheerfully, filling the room with gentle warmth. The scene seemed straight out of a fairy tale book, and Goh marveled at how it looked frozen in motion, and all that was missing were inhabitants. She could tell, by the size of one of the chairs and the other toys peeking out randomly at various spots, that one of them must be a child. She also noticed a lack of a television set.

Her nose suddenly seized on a scent, a little harder to pick up over the smell of the fire, but she recalled getting a whiff of it outside. Cinnamon. Her stomach, dissatisfied with the forging through the garden, urged her to move forward, across the room to the door to her right, which led into a kitchen. There she discovered the source of the delicious scent, sitting and still steaming on a round table.

The kitchen was larger than the living room, though only by a little bit, and the room was no less cozy. The fireplace in here was a great big stone hearth, but there was no fire in it. Most of the cooking was likely done at the small gas stove settled among the small white counters. Copper pots and pans and drying herbs hung from the exposed rafters running along the ceiling. The walls had a rustic white-washing treatment, and the round table was set aside for a dining area. The center of the table boasted a quaint little centerpiece, a fat vase stuffed with wildflowers. At three of the four spots at the table, woven place mats were arranged, and, on top of those, were big bowls of steaming porridge. Earthenware bowls, too, with a thick, neat blue stripe. Goh could tell right away this was miles away from the disgusting gruel that served as dinner in the facility; this was honest-to-goodness, stick-on-your-ribs, delicious with a dash of cinnamon and sugar porridge. There was a fleeting thought over how odd it seemed that the bowls were set out and ready as if to be eaten, but her hunger and desire overtook her sense, and she pulled out a chair and plopped herself down in front of the first bowl. She grabbed the spoon, digging it in as she pulled the bowl closer to shovel the porridge into her mouth.

Instantly, she regretted it, letting out a surprised shout of pain as the spoon clattered on the table. She left her mouth open, rolling out her tongue and waving her hand in front of her mouth before letting out a whimper. "Hot!" she moaned. "Too hot!"

She blew on the bowl, but realized the scorching temperature wasn't likely to cool down any time soon. Her attention moved to one of the other bowls, noticing that there wasn't any steam emitting from it, and so she switched the bowls, to take up the other, but she didn't get very far. When she touched the bowl, she discovered the next surprise. "Why, it's too cold!" she remarked, dipping a finger into the porridge and discovered that it might as well be iced. Giving another whimper, Goh realized she'd happily suck down the cold porridge if it meant getting fed, but there was still one more bowl to try. She frowned at it skeptically, as if she could pity it into being better than the others, and then she drew it in close, picked up the spoon and dug it into the cereal.

Her melting sigh of satisfaction could not have been happier. A second spoonful soon followed, then a third. "This is just right," she said in contentment, and the next thing she knew, the spoon was scraping the bottom of the bowl for the very last bites, and her stomach was not only full, but it was pleased as well. Leaning back in the chair with her hand on her full stomach, Goh sighed and wondered if she had ever felt this completely fulfilled before in her life. She doubted it. This feeling was just perfect.

Well...almost perfect, anyway.

Underneath her, the flat wooden seat of the kitchen chair was starting to feel a little uncomfortable. It was strange; she figured she would have been used to it, since the facility chairs weren't exactly designed for comfort. Still, she thought of how plushy the ones in the living room had looked and, with her stomach full, decided it couldn't hurt to put her feet up before she started moving again. She would just have to keep her ears open for signs that the owners of the house were returning. It seemed strange that they would leave when they had their meals all set out and ready to go, but, as Goh shuffled from the kitchen back into the living room, she didn't afford it any more thought than a passing note to herself.

Goh tried the largest and closest chair first. It was on one side, while the smaller ones sat almost adoringly across from it. Tall backed, with rich brown leather, slightly cracked but very smooth from plenty of care and use. She used the arms to help lower herself down into it; the sides and the back rose like a fortress wall around her. She felt tiny inside of it; the person who used it regularly either liked that diminishing effect or was quite large himself. She almost felt like a queen on a throne, but her butt shifted a little where she sat, her nose wrinkling. "Too hard," she murmured, realizing that the kitchen chairs had almost been more comfortable. She pulled herself back up and cut across the rug to the next chair.

This one, she noticed, was a bit of a rocking chair, but nothing like the wooden rocking chair in the living room at the facility, where some of the girls would spend hours sitting, rocking back and forth, back and forth, staring or muttering to themselves. This rocking chair seemed dedicated to the art of pillows and cushions, bloated with them, on its back, on its seat, and its round and puffy arms. The pattern was a pale yellow spotted with red flowers, and Goh regarded it with skepticism. Still, she gave it a try, taking a second to gain control over the movement, the rocking back and forth, holding it still with a foot on the floor.

Holding a foot on the floor was harder than Goh would have ever expected. She began sinking into the cushions that surrounded her, to the point where she thought she was going to be swallowed right up, and it took a few kicks of her legs to get her back and upright and back to her feet. She let out a disapproving sound, still feeling a little like she was caught in the rocking motion despite being free of the cushions.

"Way too soft," she said, wondering how anyone could ever find any of these chairs remotely comfortable. Still, she'd come into their house and eaten their food, so she supposed it was not her place to judge. The third chair was smaller still, though it seemed a good size for Goh, who was always a little on the short and petite side anyway. Best of all, it looked quite normal and quite comfortable. The design on the padding was a somewhat garish blue plaid, but it wasn't as though she had to look at it while she sat. As a matter of fact, the moment she did sit and curl up her legs comfortably, she realized that she could sit there for quite a bit happily.

"Just right," she said, with the slightest of adjustment and gave a sigh of relief to finally be sitting and comfortable and not even thinking about her current predicament.

The sigh, though, was poorly timed, at least, Goh could only assume that was the case because the moment she let it out, there was a faint creaking below her and the next thing she knew, after a sudden crack, she was sitting on the floor, bewildered and in the middle of a pile of broken chair pieces. "What the--"

She refused to believe that the integrity of the chair was so poor that her sitting there for a few minutes would cause the entire thing to break, but there she was, surrounded by the evidence. She picked up one of the chair legs out from underneath her, narrowing her eyes accusingly at it. "What a piece of shit," she said, giving it a half-hearted chuck across the room. Then, as she sat there thinking about what she was going to do next, Goh let out a long, languid yawn and realized how sleepy and tired she was. She supposed she never considered that she would have to rest eventually, or maybe she figured she would have just found shelter in the woods. Now, with the warm fire, her full stomach, and the comfort of an actual house, she started to think different. Yawning again, she considered the stairway leading upwards, into the second floor, where she was sure to find a bed, or, if anything, a few supplies to take with her on the road. She should scope the place out, look for anything useful, and then get ready to embark again, find a good camping spot, and call it a day. Using the end table for support, Goh pulled herself up to her feet, stretched out with another yawn, and started shuffling toward the stairs.

Since the lower level of the house was so small and quaint, Goh wasn't expecting much out of the second floor, either. At the top of the stairs, there was another landing, a little square with a hand-woven rug and a square window flanked by lacy red curtains. It looked out over the back of the house, the forest and the sloping hills that lead to the mountains in the distance, a pleasant little view, so it was a pity that the window was so small and restricted it as it was. There were two doors, one open into a tiny little bathroom. After helping herself to their dinner and then breaking their furniture, Goh barely thought it would be a big deal if she took a second to relieve herself, though she was thinking she almost preferred using leaves over the scented colored toilet paper that the residents of the house seemed to prefer.

As she would have guessed, the other door lead into a bedroom, but she was surprised to see that, apparently, they all shared the room and slept in three separate beds. As soon as she saw them, the exhaustion that she'd only been vaguely aware of came in and swept through with full force. She tried to remind herself that she'd only come up here to see if she could find any good supplies, but the urge to nap was overpowering. She could feel her eyelids drooping as if someone had placed weights on them; her body sagged with the anticipation of lying down.

Maybe if she just rested her eyes, just enough to recharge herself and be ready to get a lot of distance behind her after she left. A little catnap. It had been such a long day.

The first bed was the largest and closest; Goh was so overtaken with exhaustion that she wanted to flop right onto it, but she would she had to almost climb a little bit to scale it. As soon as she was there, she realized that the effort was completely wasted. That the bed had a mattress didn't seem like an appropriate description; she may as well be lying on boards! Whoever's bed this was, she assumed he or she had the privileged of the extremely hard chair downstairs, and they must have the back of a stone god. Grunting with irritation, Goh threw her legs back over the side of the bed, put her feet to the floor and pushed herself up to move over to the next one.

She should have known what was going to happen. It had the same poofy and poorly decorated feel of the chair that seemed to match its bedspread perfectly, but Goh decided to try it anyway. And then she had to spend the next five minutes trying to swim out from where she sunk deep, deep into the fluff of the mattress. When she did come up, rolling off the bed onto the floor because she couldn't manage to sit up without anything firm below her, she gasped as thought she was drowning in a sea of blankets and down.

"Too hard," she muttered to herself, brushing off her clothes as she glared at the first bed, and her hatred shifted over to the second. "Too soft. Let me guess, this next one is going to be just right."

Three seconds after she put down her head, the assessment proved true. Her irritation immediately dissipated, her exhaustion returning as she settled against the pillow with a satisfied sigh. Slowly, her eyelids started to slide down over his eyes and she breathed in deep, to let the sleep in. Just for a little bit, just a small little nap, and then she'd be off, she'd be free...

***

In a small little room, on a rolling computer chair, the doctor glanced from one screen to the other. He took careful note of the scene in green, captured by the unseen camera in the corner. The other displayed a thermal imaging of the same scene, registering the vitals of the little red blur in the center of the bed, reading her internal temperatures, the pace of her breathing, the beating of her heart. Shaking his head, hardly believing that the whole thing had actually worked, he waited for the numbers to reach the levels that indicated she had slipped completely into REM sleep. So far-fetched, but it all fell into place, just as Dr. Grimm had said it would. That was why Dr. Grimm was the expert, and they were all his little worker bees. He leaned over to press a large black button on his intercom system.

"Dr. Grimm?" he said. "Operation has reached the anticipated conclusion; the subject has reacted perfectly to the sleeping drug in the porridge and is now in the anticipated location. Doesn't look like she'll be waking up any time soon."

"Excellent," the good doctor's voice managed to fill the room with its deep timber even through the static of the radio. "Send in the Bears."

Jolene

I.

Expelling a sigh, a little breath of expired air, Jolene runs a hand through the thick mass of her black hair. Her fingers itch through it like serpents, a modern day Medusa. Vibrant, crimson lips purse elegantly, pale smoke escaping, carefully directed toward the sky. She approaches her cigarettes as if she's just stepped out of a movie, film noir, from the ranks of Hepburn and Hepburn, in all their classic decadence. She is beautiful, and she knows it, leaning against a tall, strong oak and wishing it was a tall, strong man. "Do you think," she asks, idle sensuality in her voice, "that Pete might come up for the weekend?"

"I'm not sure." Midori sits nearby, on a rock, but she has no cigarette, just a baggie of little orange carrot sticks to munch on. She's only there to keep Jolene company. "Probably. He doesn't seem to have anything better to do on the weekends."

The conversation has nowhere to go, so Jolene merely nods and returns to satisfying the little nicotine demon gnawing at her fingertips.

Simultaneously, she tries to ignore the crisp crunch of carotene in Midori's tiny mouth. It's cramping her style, really, and Midori is dull company even on a good day. You took what you could get, though.

Jolene touches the corner of her eye to eradicate her clumping mascara just in time to smile at two fine specimens of men approaching the door to the dormitory nearby. One stops, right between the girls, so the other stops as well. They are distinctly angled toward the girl with the carrots.

"Midori! Hi!"

Midori looks startled for a moment, like a small pale bird, but then she smiles, a hand flying up to cover the food in her mouth. "Oh, hi!" Her smile is bashful, and Jolene sends a shower of ash to the cement, feeling a flash of anger, feeling slighted, ignored.

"I didn't know you lived in Banning," the young man continues, a brunette twig with a prominent hipbones to keep his dark khakis up. Jolene's own hips shift, snaking hungrily to be pressed against his.

"Good old Banning." Midori smiles in a way that hides her teeth, although they already know about the carrot stuck between them, since she opens her mouth too wide when she talks. Jolene sighs with exaggerated insistence, trying to get their attention, or at the very least an introduction, but she seems to be invisible. The conversation trudges on without her.

"You guys live around here?" Midori asks.

"We're over in Carver." The other one speaks bashfully, with inexperience that makes Jolene ache. "Just here to play games with some friends." He holds up mess of cords and video game controllers in demonstration.

"Want to join us?" The first boy doesn't bother masking his hope.

"Oh, no. Thank you." Midori gives a faint laugh and the boys exchange smirks that she doesn't see. Jolene sees them, though, and, disgusted, she tosses her cigarette out for the bad taste invading her tongue. She smashes it into the sidewalk with her black, strappy sandals.

"I'm terrible at video games, anyway," Midori adds in apology, though Jolene doubts that it's sincere.

They try their best to hide their disappointment, and Jolene is now feeling bored as well as annoyed. She tries another cigarette, smoothly sliding one from the slim pack in her pocket. The boys give their awkward good-byes, and Midori nods, smiles, waving her small hand. Jolene edges over enough to peek through the window in the door to watch them as they disappear down the stairs. "Well," she decides, going to sit beside Midori on the rock, "they were cute. Who are they?"

Midori shrugs, tossing her long ponytail over her shoulder. "I don't really know the blonde one." She almost sounds surprised that someone unfamiliar would want to speak with her. "But the other one's in my math class." Searching for a name, her eyes roll back in her head slightly. "Jason, I think."

"You should introduce me sometime."

The sarcasm is completely lost on Midori. Instead of realizing her lack of manners, she expresses surprise.

"Oh, no," she shakes her head. "Jason has a girlfriend, and—"

"And the only reason I'd want to meet a guy is to sleep with him?" Jolene finishes, before Midori can even have a chance.

"No! That's not what I…mean…what I meant to say was just—"

"You know what, Midori?" Jolene sighs, running a hand through her hair again. Already, the new cigarette is starting to taste bad. "You're lucky that I can pretend. Pretend to buy that whole innocent act you've got going for you."

Midori blinks, then her eyes widen. "What do you mean by that?" she asks, finally starting to sound offended, starting to guess that perhaps Jolene isn't out here to be friends with her at the moment.

"I think you know what I mean," Jolene shifts, leaning toward the other girl. Her tongue drags across her top lip, and she bites down on the lower, soft tissue between hard teeth. "I saw how you were with those guys. You were bored. Uninterested. In them. In what's between their legs. You like something else, don't you, Midori?"

Dark eyes settle pointedly on Midori, and Jolene touches her shoulder to hers.

"Jolene!" Quickly, Midori pulls away, her voice peaking in pitch. It's a worried sound, and her forehead creases with her evident disgust. "What…what are you talking about?"

Grinning wickedly, Jolene takes back the closeness Midori tried to erase, the air around them tightening like a guitar string. She reaches over, twining the fingers of her free hand through the soft black waterfall of Midori's ponytail. "You were so shy around them," Jolene practically purrs in response to Midori's wide eyes. "Because you don't want them to know that you don't like them. Or boys at all, right?"

"What?" Reaching a pitch scarcely audible to human ears, Midori is scandalized, looking as though she doesn't know whether she wants to punch Jolene or run off and cry. Jolene is reveling in every second of it, finding the other girl's anathema for the suggestion delicious like cake.

"Why hide it?" The tip of Jolene's tiny nose hovers next to Midori's cheek. She breaths though it lightly, hot air sending twitches through Midori's smooth, pale skin. Each word Jolene speaks takes its time exploring deep, sensual emphasis. "I know, Midori. I know that underneath your perfect, preppy exterior, there's just a horny little dyke itching to get out."

"J-Jolene." Breathless, Midori can barely respond, her voice a trembling mix of fear and excitement. Jolene can taste it on the tip of her tongue. Midori tries to move away, but Jolene follows her, covering every inch. Realizing that she can't escape, Midori's eyes begin to dart around madly, searching for strength, for help, for a distraction.

And she finds it, in two approaching figures, well-timed silhouettes against the backdrop of sunset. Paper cups in hand, heavy boots on their feet, their laughter jangles like keys with each step, and Midori finds her salvation. She shoves Jolene away with inspired strength in her tiny limbs, scrambling for them with awkward steps.

"Catherine! Kenny!" Midori beams with gratitude, all smiles and bright red blushes. Jolene leans back, sucking on her cigarette to calm the dizziness of being so influential. "Hi."

Catherine seems to think nothing of Midori's exuberance, laughing with clueless amusement. Dumb fucking blonde. "Hey, Midori. Hi, Jolene."

Jolene nods politely; at least Catherine has the decency to acknowledge her. Smooth grey smoke spills past her lips. "Catherine." To Kenny, she smiles knowingly, but he just looks confused, his thick eyebrows scrunching toward his nose. "What's up?"

"The usual." Catherine shrugs, though her voice is bright with the excitement of talking. "Classes, getting coffee—"

"Watching crazy ass squirrels," Kenny adds with a dull drone, his voice devastatingly deep, rocks tumbling down a mountainside after the tinkling stream of Catherine's.

"Trying to get them to growl!" As she says it, Catherine makes it seem like the most important work ever. Forget feeding starving children in Africa, forget finding the cure for cancer. There are squirrels that need to growl.

"Growl?" Midori tilts her head.

"Yeah, they growl," Catherine explains. "It's really quiet, and you can barely hear it, and it might just be a car that I heard, but I'm pretty sure it was the squirrels growling."

"Funny as fuck," Kenny offers, monotone, emotionless. He spoke darkly, wore dark clothes; dark personified. His deep cheeks are like craters in a pale moon, creating dark shadows. A dark patch of hair on his sharp chin like healthy pubes. Sharp nose, sharp little eyes. His hair hung thickly in sharp spikes around his ears, his eyebrows, the nape of his neck. When Jolene thinks of sex with Kenny, she thinks of blades. She thinks of his sharp hipbones pressing against her, his sharp teeth digging into her shoulder.

She thinks of Midori, too. No one's eyes shone as bright with infatuation as hers did when she talked to Kenny. Jolene notices it even now, wondering if, already, Midori's forgotten about what just transpired between them. Forget possible lesbianistic persuasions; imagine the look on Midori's cheerleading sorority girlfriends' faces when they discovered that their peppy little queen got moist over skinny little goth boys.

One of these days, Jolene decides, she will fuck Kenny. For now, however, she only interrupts. She drops her cigarette, pulling up her jeans a little as she stands. "So," she says, adjusting the hem of her garment. "As fascinating as this topic is, I'm wondering if any of you planned on going to the club tonight."

Catherine smiles, blonde fucking magic sparkles in her perfect blue eyes. "Yeah. Trev says it kind of sucks, but everyone's going to be there. I'd hate to miss out on some of those youthful magic moments."

Kenny abruptly grunts, dissatisfied as he shoves his hands deep into his pockets. "Yeah, right," he says. "Ass shaking and drunk ass idiots. Can't fucking wait. Let's go inside. The sun. It burns."

Catherine laughs. Midori giggles. Jolene can't roll her eyes hard enough. "Come on, Vlad." Catherine moves, grabbing his thin arm. "Let's get you in your coffin."

Midori, of course, follows, and so Jolene does, too, and the world darkens as they pass through the doors, making their way down the stairs, through the hall. The weak light from the fluorescent bulbs overhead hurts Jolene's eyes at first; it seems like they'll never quite adjust, but they always do, just as they reach the door to their room. It's decorated extravagantly by each girl who lives inside, individual contributions with their own eclectic tastes in vain attempts to proclaim "I am unique!" Catherine has posted a bunch of flyers for bands Jolene has never even heard of and can't be bothered with keeping straight since they all sound the exact same. Midori has sketched fairies and ballerinas, and Jennifer has gathered a nauseating amount of stickers, bunnies and flowers. Jolene has put up pictures of men. Lots and lots of men.

Jolene turns the bulbous, copper-colored knob and pushes, but the door does not open. Locked. She can't help the icy grin that crosses her face. At least this answers her question if Pete was visiting this weekend.

She unlocks the thick dormitory door, like she's done one hundred times before. Jolene smoothes her dark hair in the mirror, right inside, moving like liquid, toward one of the bedroom doors. She sends a malicious glance over to her companions. Kenny is the only one to return it; the other two stare hard, daring her not to do what she's thinking. She raises her fist and brings it down hard, the deep thudding knock resonating through the room.

"Show's over, fuckfaces!" she calls out melodically. "Get your pants on!"

Sounds of chaos and annoyance instantly burst on the other side of the door, a frustrated groan and a very vocal, "Fuck you, Jolene!"

"As much as I know you'd like that, Pete," Jolene sings back triumphantly, "I don't think Jen would. Unless you're into that, Jennifer?"

"That," Kenny comments as he lazily flops onto the couch, reaching for the TV remote, "was kind of evil, Jolene." There may be a hint of approval in his voice; it's really hard to tell.

"Go watch TV in your own room, Kenny," Catherine plunges down beside him, prying the remote away. Midori joins them, Kenny now between the girls, and whispered conversation drifts from the bedroom, mingling with the sound of flipping channels. "I was so close." "We'll try again later, promise." "Fucking hate that bitch."

"Well," Jolene announces, shoulders squared with satisfaction, "I'm getting ready."

"Getting ready?" Midori frowns. "We're not leaving for another two hours."

"Barely enough time. Hope no one needs the bathroom soon." Jolene graces them all with one last smile before closing the bathroom door firmly behind her. A few moments later, once the shower has reached the right temperature, she hears Pete outside, banging on the door with a flurry of curses, and she smiles again to herself.

II.

Surrounded by chaos and flashing lights, Jolene rises above her surroundings, above the crowding swarm. Head held high, shoulders squared, her back curves perfectly. A dark goddess descending her heavenly perch to grace the mortals with her divine presence. Her black pleated skirt is flawless and short, still within the bounds of decency, though showcasing her long, spectacular legs. There's motion in the folds as she moves, perfectly choreographed with her hips. Her toes glitter as they peek slyly out of the fashionable gaps in her fuck-me pumps. Her breasts bounce, round and white, bounce like her skirt from inside the snug silken top, the one that makes her feel like a disco queen. It is barely more than a sling haltered around her neck to keep her covered. Overwhelmed by the Aphrodite inside of her, Jolene closes her eyes, tossing her head back, shaking out her hair. A soft cloud of black behind her, she breathes in deep to inhale the familiar aromas of cream rinse and tobacco smoke, a sickly scent that is always, always there.

Jolene sends a coy smile over her shoulder, at Kenny, at Pete, at any male willing to receive it as her group sails through the sea of beautiful young people. Well, not all of them are beautiful, including members of her own party, but Jolene easily dismisses them, pushes them back into a realm of nonexistence, focusing only on the specimens worth her time. The music is loud, intrusive, growling and rumbling hip-hop-rap that makes her want to grind her body against someone. She's already moving, leaning into someone she doesn't know. A friend of Catherine's? Trevor's? It doesn't matter; his body is warm and hard, and that's what counts.

But the dancing doesn't last long; most of her friends are sitting, timid, afraid. Conversation is nearly impossible without straining vocal chords, so taking in the view and making eyes at guys gets old quick. "Why are we just sitting here?" Jolene complains over the thumping bass. "You go to a dance club to dance, you guys!"

"What?" Jennifer shouts, looking to Pete as if he would have had better luck hearing it. The darkness and flashing lights make her eyes look even more lost in her round, puffy face.

Catherine hears it, though, and she laughs, though it's an embarrassed, awkward laugh. "I can't dance to this song!" she declares. "It's against my musical standards."

"Come on, Catherine," Midori offers the other girl a smile, placing a soft hand on her shoulder. Jolene quirks an eyebrow at the gesture, intentionally swiping away its innocence, and Midori quickly removes it. "It's not like they're going to play any punk or death metal in a place like this, so you might as well get it out of the way now."

"That's right," Jolene says with a nod, authoritative and all-knowing. "I'm just going to keep pestering you all night until you do."

Jennifer and Pete manage to slip away, relieving Jolene of at least one eyesore, though she can't help noticing the terrifyingly hypnotic sway of Jennifer's ass squeezed into pants at least one size too small. It's revolting, but she can't help being somewhat fascinated by the idea of a creature so disgusting being so utterly clueless. It becomes even worse when Jennifer starts to dance, if it can be called that, and she thinks, not for the first time, how a guy like Pete, with blonde hair and fucking dimples, could stand being with a massive cow like that.

"Fat people," she mutters under the tones of the music, "should not be dirty dancing."

"And people in glass houses shouldn't throw stones."

Surprised that anyone even heard her, Jolene starts, turning her head and discovering that everyone has left and she's alone at the table with Kenny. She narrows her eyes at him.

"I'm a size two, asshole."

Kenny shrugs. "Everyone went over to the dance floor while you were checking out Jen's ass."

She hardens her glare, but chooses not to respect that comment with a retort. She notices how the flickering lights create drama in his face, the dark lines of his angular features growing and shrinking while his pale skin illuminates in shifting greens, reds, blues. She glances at the crowded dance floor, where Midori is pulling a laughing and cowering Catherine into the mass of churning bodies, and her mind returns to Kenny with thoughts shifted. She's reminded of all the times she's thought about the sharpness of his features, on sex and blades and sharp, sharp teeth, on how she's vowed to herself that, one day, she would fuck him. With Catherine and Midori distracted, perhaps this is that day.

"Why aren't you out there, too?" she asks, smiling as sweetly as she can while reaching into her purse for a pack of cigarettes. She slides one out, slowly, deliberately. She then finds her lighter, flicking it open after the cigarette rests between her lips. She sets the end to a soft, glowing ember.

"You're kidding, right?" He looks over at Jolene through his shaggy hair, his tongue pressing against the sharpness of his teeth. His eyes shift slightly, briefly, to the deep crease of cleavage created by the position of Jolene's arms, and then they seem to affix on her cigarette.

Considering the dark hair, the dark clothing, a hint of dark make-up, dark, dark, dark all over Kenny, Jolene smirks. "Okay, yeah, I guess you're not much of a dancer, right? So then why are you in a dance club?"

"Catherine asked me to come," he answers, sliding his eyes toward the dance floor again, toward Catherine and her long, swaying blonde hair, her dark tartan skirt, a little too short.

Jolene takes another long, deep drag of her cigarette and brushes a few ashes off the table.

"What's with that, anyway?" she asks. "You and her. Are you guys, like, a thing?"

He hits her with a glare. She blinks, surprised that a pair of eyes could feel so much like a slap. "She's my best friend," he says, "since practically kindergarten. What's it to you?"

"Just wondering. You two confuse me, I guess. I mean, she acts all virginal and shit, but the way you two are always together, I figured…"

"It's not all about fucking, Jolene. I love Catherine like a sister. Not an actual sister, mind you. I can't fucking stand my actual sister."

Jolene lets out another slow plume of smoke, tilting her head. Her eyes narrow as she tries to decipher what he means, but she can't picture the two of them in a platonic sense at all.

"What?" Kenny seems affronted by her lack of understanding. "Don't you have a friend or a sister or someone you're that close to?"

She doesn't, and Jolene exists, for a moment, in silence. Faintly, the silence is replaced with singing. Not the voices over synthesized beats and melodies, but the soft song of crickets, singing in the forest. It is only there for a moment, brief enough to disappear as soon as it came, the loud club returning. "No," she says, almost too quiet for Kenny to hear. "No, I don't.

"And I don't understand it, either," she continues, coming back with intensity. "I don't fucking get it. How come everyone else seems to have something, except me? You and Catherine.

Everyone fucking loves Midori. And even Jennifer, that fat fucking pig, has someone! What the fuck?"

"Why the hell are you just sitting here talking to me, anyway?" Kenny, probably not knowing what else to say, tilts his head back. "I didn't mean to get you all fucking sad and upset, but I'm depressing as hell. You're the one who loves this sort of a shit, so get out there."

Jolene snorts a laugh, an unbecoming sound, but she can't help it. "You're right," she says, feigning humor, though she feels plagued and confused inside. She turns on her most charming smile as she asks, "Gonna dance with me, Kenny?"

Kenny snorts back. "Fuck, no. Over my dead corpse. I don't dance."

"Your loss!" Jolene nearly sings it as, smiling, she slides off the stool in search of a more willing partner. She takes a moment, sniffing, to brush a finger under her eyes, and she locates a table filled with eligible-seeming young men. If anything, one of them will dance with her. There are five of them, all laughing and talking over their drinks. Older guys, which boosts their appeal significantly. She clears her throat and saunters over.

"I'm sorry to interrupt, fellas," she starts with a smile, brightening her eyes with intensity as she looks them over them and a new song starts up, "but I'm without a dance partner, and I can't miss this song."

As she expects, they are impressed that a girl is willing to make the first move or are, at the very least, very good at pretending to be impressed. They exchange a glance, sending secret messages with their eyes, until one, grinning in victory, breaks it off with a laugh. He slides out of his chair to stand, only a little taller than Jolene, generally average, brown hair, hazel eyes. He has a killer smile, though, and Jolene matches it as she grabs his hands and drags him toward the dance floor. "Let's go."

The anonymous dancing recharges Jolene. The sharp energy of letting the music take over, letting hormones and the driving beat control her every move makes her head swim. There's the touching, the grinding, the seemingly casual groping. She's starting to sweat; he's slick with perspiration, too, and she runs a hand through his damp mop of hair before seductively twisting down. She moves back up in one continuous, sinuous motion. He whispers something in her ear; she can't hear what it is over the loud music, but she laughs anyway, throwing back her head. He leans in toward her elongated neck and pulls her in close, groins pressed together.

Briefly, Jolene sends her eyes around the floor, looking for the others. Midori must have made up a little dance and shared it with Catherine, because they are both laughing as they move in unison. A stupid thing, half line dance, half showman's jazz. They're oblivious to the world around them, not seeming to care that they don't look in the least bit sexy, nothing like the girls in short skirts and halters surrounding them. A pang of envy stabs Jolene somewhere in her left side, but she ignores it. She's the one out here dancing with a hot older guy, his hands firm on her hips, his mouth dangerously close to her ear.

Then Jolene spots Jennifer and Pete, and the disgusting display that is Jennifer's attempt to dance. The pang is driven in deeper, and now it causes nausea. It isn't just that Jennifer is fat, but that she is fat and ugly, inside and out. At least Jolene is beautiful on the outside. Selfish, stupid, dependant. Jolene is already sick of having to overhear all of her late-night telephone arguments, the whining and the demands. Pete seems like such a great guy, cute and sensitive and, from what Jolene can glean, pretty good in bed, too. Yet he was wasting all that talent on a some stupid bitch with an ass as dense as her brain. He's up close against her, bodies rubbing together, simulating sex.

Jolene almost loses her balance. Almost as if on call, Pete looks over, catching her stern observation of him and the supposed love of his life. Her eyes grow wide, but, to her surprise, he smiles. Intrigued, Jolene notices that Jennifer is too absorbed in her own world to notice much else, so her anger quickly manifests into diabolical desire. She smiles back.

Jolene knows that Pete is now watching her, and she also realizes that he is aware of her intentions. He's a smart boy, knows exactly what's on her mind. It makes her want to laugh. She can see it in his eyes, locked onto her form as she continues to grind with her unknown partner, her hips moving exaggeratedly with the words of the song, nice and slow so he can follow her every move.

"Hey!" She breaks from the mental ravishing as the song changes, shouting loudly and sending Pete a meaningful glance in case she can't hear her talking to the young man she dragged away from his friends. "Thanks. I'm going to step outside, get some fresh air."

Jolene doesn't even hear what he says, but she catches the question in his tone and the hopeful look in his eyes. She grins, running a finger down his chest. "Absolutely," she says, swishing her hair as she turns and performs her much-practiced strut toward the door.

The air feels great, cool and intoxicating after the heat of the club. With nervous little fingers, Jolene adjusts her clothes. Brushes a hand through her hair, straightens her skirt, wipes the sweat from her forehead. He'll take his time, to be less conspicuous. Her heels click on the sidewalk as she makes it towards the back of the building. The quiet, secluded little alleyway with its lone, yellow sodium light.

Just as she's about to get bored and return inside, Pete appears, breathless, his shirt partially unbuttoned. "Jolene!"

"Oh!" Jolene jumps, hand flitting to her chest. "Pete! You scared me half to death!"

He laughs, leaning over her with his hand pressed against the wall beside them. It traps her in. "Come on, Jolene. I know you didn't come out here just for a breather."

"Sure I did." Jolene feigns confusion, shaking her head slightly as she frowns. Her hand waves in front of her, as if to cool herself off. "It's too crowded in there."

Again, he laughs, and Jolene starts to push past him to walk away. But he grabs her arm and pulls her back. A shiver of excitement runs through her for a moment, and then she remembers to struggle a little bit.

"I saw the way you were looking at me, Jolene." Pete stares at her, eyes bright and intense, and his grip tightens on her arm. "I know what that look means."

"Let go of me," she says, trying to wrench her arm free, which she knows is futile. "What are you even talking about?"

"Don't play me, Jolene." He pulls her into him, pressing his body against her, pelvis to pelvis, a move that always makes her knees weaken. She can feel him against her leg; he feels like a big boy, and she can't wait. "I know you want me. Ever since you met me, and you can't stand that I'm with Jen."

"Pete!" Jolene doesn't even bother putting strength into her shove, and she knows that her shrill objection doesn't sound convincing. "Let me go! You are so full of shi—"

His mouth against hers cuts her off, his lips pressing hard, his tongue probing with hunger. Jolene remembers again to struggle against him, make it seem like she doesn't want it while every inch of her cries out in glorious euphoria. His hand starts sliding up her skirt; she pushes it away. It returns hastily, pushing aside her barely-there lace thong, and his fingers slowly start massaging, massaging, and then digging into her, deep and forceful. She lets out a cry of surprise, silenced again by his insistent tongue. He knows what he's doing, managing to work her with one hand while the other unzips his jeans, and, before she knows it, he's plunging himself deep inside of her, not as big as she had imagined. But it still feels good, though she pretends it doesn't. Pete murmurs his angry grunts and taunts into her ear. She forgets to fight, digging her fingers into his back, left leg lifted to wrap around him. Right then, she knows there must be something more. There must be something more than the lust, the desire, the sex. But it's all she has at the moment, so she clings tighter to his sweating body.

For a second, it all fades away. Jolene feels numbs, hears nothing until a gentle sound swells, her father's uneven snores. Singing in the forest. Slowly, the strange sounds cease, and sirens take their place, blaring in her head. Just a passing ambulance, the pumping music from behind her on the wall against her back, and Pete's rhythmic rumbles. She feels the spasm of orgasm racing through her body, pulsating between her legs, filling her with uncontrollable ecstasy. Jolene tilts back her head and feels the tears rolling down her cheeks.

There must be something more.

Spider and Fly

Listening to Mrs. Halloran tell the ancient tale of Arachne, Ariana couldn't help smile to herself. She imagined the young Greek maiden with her fingers at the loom, working away at her thread to create a tapestry to best the goddess Athena, and she felt her own hands move as if weaving with her, spinning out threads with her skin tingling and her eyes closed. In the end of the story, Mrs. Halloran said that Athena turned Arachne into a spider to punish her, but Ariana knew that being a spider was no punishment. It was a gift.

For the most part, Ariana had stopped paying much attention to Mrs. Halloran, like most of the other students in her third period Language Arts class. It was considered, by and large, a blow-off class, and it didn't help that it was placed right smack before lunch period, either. She mostly didn't bother because she found most of what the teacher had to say to be boring or contrite, especially now that they were into mythologies. It was always Greek mythology, too, none of the fun ones that showed the spider for what it truly was, clever, industrious, a trickster.

With her pencil tapping lightly on her desk, Ariana started to hum a little under her breath. *Come into my parlor, said the spider to the fly…* She rehearsed the words of her favorite poem through her head as she thought about the end of the day, where she'd go home, finish her work, the story of Arachne only making her itch to get back to her spinning, see what kind of flies she could catch.

Come into my parlor.

***

Luke found it impossible to listen to Mrs. Halloran in class, and he was glad that third period Language Arts was the only class he had with Ariana Spinnt. Otherwise, he would probably be failing out of high school entirely. He had been assigned a place three seats over and three seats back from Ariana, giving him a perfect view of her in quarter-profile, enough to see her impossibly fair, pink face, to get the full effect of her long dark hair, always intricately braided, and he got just enough of that distant smile that always seemed to be on her face. He couldn't imagine it had anything to do with the lesson, something about Greek gods and spiders and weaving, but whatever had made Ariana smile like that, he wanted to know what it was. It was so blissful, and her eyes held a distant shimmer to them that said she was in her own world. He wanted to be in that world with her.

She was humming, too. He could just barely hear it, and even the mysterious song was enticing. Sometimes Luke entertained the idea that Ariana might be thinking about him, but he doubted it. She probably didn't even know he existed. He never spoke in class unless he absolutely had to, and she sat in front of him, so it wasn't like she would ever see him, unless he was entering the room, leaving it, or completely mortifying himself whenever they had to make oral presentations. He always looked into the crowd, to see if she was watching him, but even then, she seemed elsewhere, much to his mutual dismay and relief.

Luke found himself tapping his fingers in thought on his desk, trying to weave together a plan. Ariana would never know who he was unless he manned up and talked to her. His eyes danced to the clock, and he caught his lower lip nervously between his teeth. Lunch was next hour. Maybe he could catch her on the way to lunch, or while she was there, that might be better, because then she couldn't escape as easily into the crowds filling into the busy hallways...

"Mr. Wing." Mrs. Halloran's voice cut sharply through his reverie, pulling out of her droning lecture with a snap that demanded his attention, as well as the attention of everyone in class. "The hour is not over yet. If I could have your attention for just ten more minutes, I might even consider going a little easier on everyone's homework this evening."

Sinking into his chair as if that could help him dive under the swell of embarrassment, Luke drew in a deep breath. "Yes, Mrs. Halloran, sorry."

She affixed him with a warning look before turning back to the board and back to her droning words. A few of the other students shook their heads at him and made it clear that if he earned them a harsher sentence, his butt was mulch. Pete Fox even threw a wad of paper at him, but that was expected of Pete.

Ariana Spinnt didn't even seem to notice. She remained wrapped up in her own little secret world, a world where there was probably only room for one.

***

The tales in class had sparked Ariana's imagination, making her eager to get through the rest of the day. This excitement was the only thing that let her survive the cafeteria at lunchtime. All that hustling and bustling, the loud noises of hundreds of voices mingling together after suffering through several hours of having to hold their tongues, the cafeteria reminded Ariana of nothing so much as a beehive, filled with mindless drones going about their mindless tasks, and it was disgusting. It was no wonder that most insects fell prey to higher, better creatures, that they would constantly get stuck in the webs weaved by others.

She had absolutely no interest in joining them. She always ate her lunch, meager as it was, at a table out of the way, closer to the kitchen, where no one ever wanted to sit if they could help it. She had a few friends she knew from this or from that, and they joined her, though they mostly kept quiet, munching contentedly, or sometimes they'd chat a little bit about a dance that was coming up or whether or not certain signals meant that the crush of the week might actually be interested. Television shows, recent movies, things like that. Tegan, scholarly and smart, would always try to bring up books, though those conversations never went far. Ariana probably liked Tegan best out of the other girls; maybe one day she should invite her over.

When Luke Wing approached the table, though, a decided silence settled over the girls. Ariana could see hesitation in the way he carried himself, a fidgeting desire to just turn and flit away after he had made progress. It looked like he was going to retreat at least three times, and she found this nervous dance intriguing. She even smiled a little. She'd never noticed how bright his small dark eyes were or how soft his cropped dark hair seemed to be. She found herself sitting up straighter, pulling up her spine to rise above her friends and make herself seem more regal and refined than those in her company. He sat behind her in Language Arts; it seemed that all the more attractive boys sat in the back of the room, but so did less academically inclined boys. He was probably coming over to pester one of them about helping with class.

When he finally stood in front of them, hands shoved awkwardly into the front pockets of his jeans, he offered an uncertain smile.

"Hey," he said.

"Hey," chorused the girls at the table, all except for Ariana, who fixed a cool, steady, appraising look on him. She was pleased to discover that this made him fidget even more. They all waited to see the reason for his visit.

"So, um, I'm sorry if this is weird," he started, staggering a little at first, but, once he got those words out, it seemed there was no going back, "but, Ariana, I sit behind you in Mrs. Halloran's class."

Her friends' eyes swiveled eagerly toward her to see how she'd react. Wiping the smile off her face, she tossed her head a little, shaking her braid over her shoulder and smoothing it out. "I know who you are," she said.

"Oh, good." Relief seemed to wash over him, relaxing him a little. "Cool. I mean, you get good grades in that class, yeah? Because, well, I'm struggling a little, and I don't think it's going to get any better once we get into all these Greek myths. You any good with that stuff?"

"Mythology's my favorite," Ariana admitted, her head tilting curiously. There was a good chance that word had gotten out that she knew her stuff when it came to myths and stories, and that Luke was legitimately there for her help. But she couldn't help wonder, or almost hoping, that it might be something else, and a plan started to develop inside of her head. "Why? Do you need help?"

"I thought it could be kind of cool if you could," he offered, sounding hopeful now, and she noticed flecks of green in his bright, eager eyes. She wanted to laugh, but she kept her demeanor calm and nonchalant with a shrug of her shoulders.

"Sure," she said. "I'd be glad to. You're not doing anything tonight, are you? I mean, if you can get an early start on some of it, you can be ahead of the game. Then maybe Mrs. Halloran will stop yelling at you in class."

Luke's face flushed a faint red, but he took the little jab in stride. "Not all of us are on her good side and can just space out in class whenever," he stabbed back, and it was just the kind of response Ariana wanted to hear. It wasn't any fun if they were too nervous and docile. She could tell Luke had some real strength about him, and she nodded her approval.

"Swing by my house later tonight," she said, swiping up a napkin and grabbing a pen so she could write the address down. "Maybe six? We can have a little tutoring session."

Luke's weight shifted from one foot to the other as Ariana scribbled out the information, but he knew to wait a second before taking it once she offered it out. He looked down at the address, her phone number, and nodded slightly. "Cool," he said, grinning. "Cool."

***

The rest of the day stretched out, impossibly long, the same three hours as usual seeming to double in length as Luke sat anxiously through his remaining classes. Crumpled up in his pocket was the napkin with Ariana's address on it, and all he could think about was the leisurely walk he would take until he found himself at her house. She'd invite him in, maybe her mother would have prepared snacks, or, even better, maybe her parents wouldn't even be home, and it wouldn't be long until they moved away from Greek mythology into more interesting topics, ones involving hands and skin and lips.

The eventual end of his classes came, gloriously, and the day was still warm and pleasant to make his walk to Ariana's house a good one, filled with thoughts of her red lips and sly smile. The perceived pleasantness of the journey was interrupted roughly, though, by an elbow in his rib, thrown by Pete Fox. Luke hadn't even seen him coming, and he blushed faintly to realize that he had been so distracted that he hadn't noticed a whole flock of his friends coming up the sidewalk and approaching him.

"Where you heading, Luke?" Pete asked, with a plaintive expression that suggested he already knew the answer. "I thought you lived down the other way."

"He does," Chris Stark chimed in, almost as if reciting a line, and Luke groaned, realizing that they had all planned the interlude. "I think he's actually heading somewhere else."

"Somewhere else?" Pete's look of confusion grew, but his grin was threatening to surface. "Like where?"

"Shut up, Pete," Luke said, fixing a warning look on the other boy, sometimes his friend but mostly just a pain in his ass.

"No, I'm really curious now," Pete persisted. "Where could old Luke be going after school on this fine day? It wouldn't have anything to do with a certain napkin at lunch time, would it?"

Pete had moved to block Luke's path, but Luke threw his shoulder forward and plowed ahead. "I don't know what you're talking about," he insisted, determined to keep going and leaving those jerks behind. They were just being jealous and petty, and he didn't have time to deal with their immaturity right now.

"I think he might actually be going to see the freak girl."

Luke stopped in his tracks. He spun around, fists clenched at his side, his eyes narrowed in warning. "She's not a freak," he said. "And so what if I am going to see her?"

"She is a freak," Pete insisted, with an unblinking firmness that showed he wasn't going to be swayed. "She has no friends, she dresses weird, and she talks to herself all the time. That humming she does? Creepy as hell. And have you ever notice that she's always twitching her fingers? It's weird."

"You seem to pay a lot of attention to what she does," Luke pointed out, "for thinking she's such a freak."

"Shut up, Luke. I just keep an eye out for the ones that are most likely to snap some day. You can't go over there, man. Are you crazy?"

And the fact of the matter was that he was crazy, crazy for Ariana, and he wouldn't expect his friends to understand something like that. In fact, he knew that if he tried to explain it, the taunts would only get worse. "Listen," he said. "Leave me alone, okay? I'm just going over there so she can help me with some stuff for class. That's it. My grades are nearly perfect except for that class, and she's really good."

"You are such a nerd," Pete said, shaking his head. "I guess this means if you get less than perfect this semester, we'll know the problem was that you guys were too busy studying anatomy when you were supposed to be studying language arts."

Feigning disgust, hoping the red in his face came off more as anger and irritation than anything else, Luke pushed past Pete again and continued walking. "Whatever, man," he said. "Leave me alone."

Pete called out after Luke one more time, while the others started to retreat with smirks and laughter. "Don't say I didn't warn you, Luke! That chick is a freak, I'm telling you."

"Shows what you know," Luke muttered to himself, turning the corner to start walking up the tree-lined street on which Ariana lived with his hands shoved into his front pockets.

"Nice knowing you, pal," Pete offered, before the two of them disappeared in the opposite directions.

***

Though she was expecting Luke at any minute, Ariana was up in her room, hard at work. She had spent a great deal of her free time weaving and weaving, but it was the first time in a long time that she intended to actually catch something in one of her webs. It stretched all across her bedroom, shimmering in an intricate pattern that she was certain would make lesser artists weep. What did the mere works of humans have that could possibly compare to something like this? Arachne was lucky; Athena had given her a gift by turning her into a spider, the same gift that Ariana had, sitting in a corner of her room, eight limbs deftly moving as she made her web stronger, better, even more beautiful.

It was a little heartbreaking to think that, once her fly had entered her parlor, his awkward limbs and flailing attempts to escape would tear her masterpiece down; it would wrap around him as he pulled, immobilizing him, so that she could descend and feed.

A little heartbreaking, but not too bad. She would always have time to build another web, for the next unsuspecting fly.

Downstairs, the doorbell rang, and Ariana heard her mother moving to answer the door. Crawling down from her web, she started to hum, and she smiled.

9 September 1976

News that Chairman Mao had died reached the village, and Lin's mother started crying. She cried hard and long, enough to fill a bucket twice over, and Lin was confused. Her mother had always muttered such terrible things about Chairman Mao; Lin thought her mother hated him and couldn't understand the reason for so many tears.

Lin's father rolled a cigarette as fat as his large fingers, went outside, and then laughed and laughed and laughed. He laughed hard and long, enough to fill the air and rattle the wind chimes and that made Lin's mother cry even harder.

Much later, when Lin realized that her stomach was full for the first time in her life, she understood why.

Bridge Over the River Yuanfen

Chen and his friends reclined on the railing of the bridge every afternoon and, every afternoon, a girl would walk across it. She had her hand wrapped around the arm of a boy and, when they reached the other side, she would sigh, a pleasant sound, like the wind in the leaves, and rest her head on his shoulders.

Every afternoon, Chen said to his friends, "I will marry that girl one day. It is destiny." They pinched and jeered and spat; a girl like that would not want an ugly pig like Chen, especially not when she already had her hand wrapped around the arm of a boy, an arm with a red band on it, and all he had were new plastic sandals.

And every afternoon, when the girl reached the other side of the bridge, she would sigh and smile and rest her head on her brother's shoulder. "Did you see that boy with the plastic sandals, brother?" she'd ask. "I will marry that boy one day. It is fate."

Spring Thaw

We were in those first early days of spring, when the world slowly warmed by the lazy heat of a pale sun, and the trees were budding with the yellow-green promise of things to come. It had been a little over a full year since the tragedy, and things were starting to finally settle into some semblance of how things used to be. In a place like this, it was easy to forget that anything had happened at all, if only for a little bit, until you emerged from the woods, back into the devastating reminders that filled every moment. She sat on a heavy slab of cement, which was slowly being overtaken by the nature around it, confirming its prominence and strength. Her legs were tucked up, chin resting on her knees, and she tilted her head as she looked at me. I was writing, pen scratching across the paper, the wind ruffling my hair. She didn't hesitate to interrupt my flow.

"Duncan?"

"Yes?"

"What used to be here, anyway?"

I glanced over at her for a moment, as she brushed a long strand of red hair from her face. Then I glanced around at all the chunks of rubble and cement scattered around us. Formidable, they poked out of the green hill like industrial thorns, some looking too random to have been anything but dumped there, but others so particularly formed that they hinted at a previous life that seemed miles away from the pastoral landscape moving in around it.

"A building, probably."

Her frown made it clear that this answer was unsatisfying. "You think so?" she asked, casting dark, doubtful eyes my way.

"Sure. I mean, look at that corner piece."

"What kind of building?"

"Probably just storage."

Her frown pulled down even more, petulance turning into annoyance, and I started to frown myself.

"What?"

"Storage?" Her voice was laced with contempt. "All the way out here?"

I shrugged. "Why not? What else could it be?"

"I don't know!" She sighed, huffing out air, her small hands flying upwards before falling limply to her side. She stretched out her legs, leaning forward. "Something more interesting than that. This place…this spot. It feels too special and interesting to have just been a storage shed."

"It's too small to be anything else," I pointed out, and had to ask, again, "What else would it be?"

"I don't know!" she said, meeting my repetition with some of her own. "You're the writer! Make something up!"

Those words were spat out with so much flippant contempt that I had no choice but to be bound by them. Holding back a sigh, I stopped my pen and tucked it behind my ear; my notebook rested on my knees, and my arms rested on my notebook. I regarded her a moment before making up my mind.

"Guard towers," I decided.

Her face was incredulous, but she laughed. "What?"

"Guard towers," I said again with an assuring nod. "For the hospital. That's why they're so far out here. They mark the parameters of the grounds, and men would be stationed here to make sure none of the loonies or psychopaths escaped."

It was incredible, the look on her face, and how she sat there, demanding tall tales, then proceed to be believe every word of them. "Really?" she asked, looking up to where these imagined towers might reach. "Did so many of them escape that they needed to post guards and everything?"

I nodded again, solemnly, marveling at how brightly her gullibility lit up her face. It made the sun filtering through trees even more atmospheric, as if dropping us into our own picture book. "Tons," I informed her. "In fact, just down that way, you can see a spot where they had to fill in the mouth of a tunnel where they were known to escape through. Legend has it that they actually filled it in with people still inside. From that point on, nobody wanted the guard duty because of all the strange things that started to happen, attributed to the restless souls of those trapped patients."

Her eyes were wide and blue and fathomless. "Really?"

"No."

He hand went flying for my shoulder. The smack didn't hurt at all, but I rubbed at it gingerly to appease her. She sulked, and I told her, simply, "You shouldn't have asked."

"Maybe it's still true," she maintained petulantly. "I mean, it's reasonable, isn't it?"

"Sure," I agreed easily enough, "but unlikely. If something like that had really happened, we'd have heard about it somewhere, you'd think."

"Maybe it's just been covered up, really well."

I was known for my cynicism, so my natural reaction was to argue with her, but the intrigue of a point like that halted my disagreement. I started to ponder the possibility. How hard would it be to create a cover for something like that, the story I had just made up right there on the spot? My brain supplied on avenue to investigate this deeper.

"Let's check it out."

"Check what out? There's a tunnel? I thought you made that up."

"I may have," I admitted, "but I did base it on a real spot out here." I started to gather my things, slipping my notebook into my bag and swinging it over my shoulders as I stood. I offered my hand. "Come on. I'm tired of just sitting here, anyway."

I pulled her easily to her feet, and we began to walk again, down the wide trails and the narrowed trails both, intentional and unintentional meanderings through the trees. They had idyllic names attached to them still, color-coded with wooden, ivy-laced sign posts. Cedar Cathedral, where the branches bent overhead in a natural tunnel. Old Orchard, where the hill sloped gently upwards and any hints of fruit-bearing trees had all together disappeared to make way for larger ones. Dagger Ridge, steep and littered with rocks. As we got closer to the old hospital grounds, the names grew increasingly clinical. Cistern Loop, twining around the big cement reservoir on the hill. Supply Line, with its two tracks dug out by trucks that once rumbled over it. Even Bathhouse Lane, where the short, overgrown road once lead to where patients would bath in the small lake.

We skirted the wide, outside paths around the grounds, drifting along the base of one of the larger hills until we finally reached the place I had mentioned. It was much further back than I had remembered, but it was still marked by a particularly stout and thick tree, its branches twisting outwards around a flat, stump-like center. "The Portal Tree," I told her, grinning as I wrapped my hand around one of the branches and dangled lightly from it.

"The what?"

"Portal Tree," I repeated, then nodded toward the center, that flat platform of a stump from which all the branches seemed to radiate. "Look at that. Too perfect to be natural."

"You mean someone made it like that?"

"Or something."

"What?"

"Not natural, but maybe supernatural. You know I like to sit on rocks and branches and logs and things when I'm writing, but you'll never catch me sitting there."

"Why not?"

"It's a Portal Tree. As in a portal to another dimension. Another world. Sit there too long, and the fairies will claim you and drag you into their nightmarish kingdom."

She shook her head. "You are so full of it."

"Am I? Fine, then. Let's take a break. Why don't you have a seat?"

Her hesitant pause was long and distressed. "I thought you were going to show me the tunnel," she finally said.

"I am." Grinning, I pointed to the hillside beyond the tree. Some of it was now reinforced by a barricade of round logs, to prevent erosion and landslides. In the vague frame of construction, with the right amount of imagination, it was easy to see how a certain spot could be the suggestion of the opening of a tunnel, filled in and grown over with grass over the years. "There. See it?"

She looked, her head tilting, spilling hair past her shoulder like a waterfall. I couldn't see her face, but I could sense the moment of recognition in her body, filling me with a grim satisfaction. Then she started to move forward, just a little, before stopping with uncertainty and glancing back at me. "There?" she asked, waiting for my affirming nod before wading through the low ferns and long wispy grass to get even closer. Shoving my hands into my pockets, I followed, appreciating the sun in her hair and the way her cautious crouch provided me with an exceptional view of her backside.

She placed a hand lightly against a post, half embedded into the hillside, which could have been the suggestion of an entrance if you opened your imagination to the suggestion. More likely, it was just an unfinished part of the erosion project, one of many projects gone fallen to the wayside in the light of the events of the past years. "Here?" she asked. Her voice was quiet, awed; it was clear that her opinion of the faint little outline was the former rather than the latter. "Oh, wow. You didn't make it up after all?"

"Maybe," I said, lifting my eyebrows speculatively. I saw her take in a deep breath of anticipation, and I couldn't keep up the farce anymore. I had to laugh, and she looked at me with irritation now replacing the wonder.

"What?" she demanded.

"Don't you think," I offered, "a secret tunnel would be a lot better hidden than that?"

She stared at me a moment as if caught in headlight, then let out a frustrated little sound. She'd have hit me, I'm sure, if I was close enough, but since I wasn't, I was able to laugh, unmolested.

"You are making this all up, aren't you?" she accused.

"Isn't that what you asked for?"

"Yeah, I guess." She fell into sulking again, her lips drawn down into a pout. I wanted to kiss them, lightly, in apology, wrap my arms around her and kiss her some more. When I reached out for her, though, her attentions were already diverted elsewhere, and she moved, slipping right out of my grasp. She was heading to the left, toward a patch of thick brush, long grass mingling with tall, overgrown brambles.

"But," she said, cautiously, carefully, "it's still entirely possible, isn't it? I mean, why not? You'd just have to look for it a little more than that."

There was something strange in her voice that made me eye her curiously. "What do you mean?"

She was already moving, though, ducking low as she gently pushed aside the waxy, thorny twists of underbrush. I went after her, wondering as the thorns caught my skin, how she'd managed to avoid being pricked. She wasn't the type to keep quiet at little painful nuisances like that. She was leading me along the base of the hill, where the trees thickened, and it started to take a real effort to continue. "Hold on," I pleaded. "It's too dense."

She wasn't listening, though. She seemed able to move with surprising ease despite the obstacles with which I was struggling. I was breathless, feeling as though every inch of exposed skin was scratched to shreds by the time I caught up with her. The brambles broke into a small hollow, like a cave, and her grin was as bright as the slanting shaft of sunlight breaking through the foliage.

"Look," she said and pointed.

I followed her finger to a small indentation there in the near vertical side of this part of the hill. About as tall as my thighs, it did look like a little archway, packed in with dirt, framed by creeping ivy.

I could only stare. "How did you…?"

She met my surprise with a chuckle and a shrug. "Intuition, I guess. You said it would have to be better hidden than that other one, so I just got the urge…I mean, look at it! That's got to be it. What else could it be?"

"Hobbit hole?"

"What's that?"

Sometimes I wondered how we were even together. It's interesting, how survival can lead the most unlikely people to each other. "I swear, I made that tunnel story up," I told her.

"Or maybe you really heard it somewhere and forgot."

I wasn't exactly convinced, but she was moving again, crouching down in front of her discovery. "How deep do you think the blockage goes?" she asked, her fingers tracing lines in the black dirt.

"Probably pretty deep if the story's true and they buried people," I offered, before I could stop myself. The whole thing was ridiculous, a mere coincidence, but I could never stop pushing her buttons.

"Maybe they weren't buried," she mused back. "Just blocked in."

My frown deepened as she started to dig into the dirt, her fingernails already darkening. An uneasy feeling started to creep over me, and her digging became more dedicated. I wanted her to stop; I was uncomfortable, and I could just tell that something was wrong. "Even if they weren't buried," I found a pleading tone in my voice, "the dirt's not going to be shallow enough that you can just dig through it. If it was, they could have dug out themselves."

That caused her to pause for a moment, and a silence settled, so much so that even the birds seemed to cease their chirping. I may have imagined it, though, taken by the tension that tightened my entire body.

"Erosion," she finally said.

"What?"

"Erosion," she repeated. "Maybe some of it's been washed away. It's been nearly a century since the hospital was operating, right? That's a lot of rain. And you saw the barriers they started putting up. Obviously, there's an erosion problem here, so maybe erosion has taken away some of the dirt."

"I'm not sure that's really how it works," I informed her, tempted to hold my stomach for all the butterflies and flip-flops it was deciding to perform. She wasn't listening, either, digging her hands in deeper. Soil coated them to her wrists, black like gloves, and she wiped them futilely on her jeans. And then back to digging again, deeper and deeper.

"Come on," I goaded, "it's a goddamn hill. You could dig forever and not get anywhere."

"Just a little bit more," she said. "If it still goes nowhere, I'll stop."

"If you're going to do this, we should at least get a shovel."

"Just a little bit more!"

I realized just then that her progress was pretty astounding. She'd managed to hollow out most of the frame, her head dipping into the round hole she'd dug. When she pulled out of the little enclave she'd created, she swiped the back of her hand across her sweating forehead, leaving a dark smear. She grinned at me, and my disquiet pitched into overdrive, striking me hard like a punch to the gut. This was a girl who complained for a week if she got a mascara smudge on her collar, and here she was, smearing soil on her face, messing up her knock-off designer jeans, and grinning about it. She seemed to be enjoying digging into the hillside with her nails, like a wild creature tearing out the bowels of its prey.

"Stop," I said. "I think we should head back."

"Just a moment! Just a little further."

"You aren't going to get anywhere!"

"At least let me try!"

"I made that story up!"

"But the archway…"

"It's probably just an old fox hole. Come on!"

"A little more!"

"It doesn't go anywhere. You'll be digging forever."

"Not if you help."

"I'm not helping."

A frustrated whine wiggled out of her. "Come on! Fine, how about this? You help me for just a few minutes, and if it still doesn't go anywhere, we'll stop, okay?"

So I started to help, if it meant that this farce would shortly be over. I couldn't help marveling at how the damp dirt just seemed to fall away at my fingertips, no matter how deep we got. We could almost fit our torsos entirely into the little cave she'd created, mounts of displaced dirt heaping at our knees. Inside, it was cool and quiet, the scent of earth and decay surrounding us like a pleasant embrace. It was like being in the womb of the world. I started to understand why she was so eager; I could feel it now, too, as I reached out and squeezed my fingers around the clumps of moist dirt, pulling them away with wispy roots and the occasional earth worm.

Then I reached out and my fingers found not the soft resistance of the soil, but the emptiness of air behind it.

"Oh my God."

She must have discovered the same thing, because she let out a triumphant laugh. "I told you, I told you! It's the tunnel! Your story was right!"

Incessantly, we dug even harder than before, eager to tear back what little else remained as quickly as possible, until we found our way through. It struck me hard just how far we had dug; both of us had to crawl a little to get into the opening space ahead, an impossible distance for how long it felt like we had been digging. But, no…the shadows outside had elongated, slanting differently, to suggest that it had been hours since we started digging. A deep exhaustion took over me, but she seemed energized by the discovery. She wriggled through the opening, straightening up in the taller inner tunnel beyond.

She looked around in astonishment, though it was too dark to see much. "Wow."

Damp, dark, dirty. The rush of the digging subsiding, all I wanted was a shower.

"It's a surprise it hasn't caved in at all," I noted, placing a hand on the side of the tunnel. It was definitely dirt, but hard as rocks, a complete contrast to the soft soil we'd come through.

"It's incredible! Do you really think it goes all the way to the hospital?"

"There's no way it's all still intact."

"We could find out!"

"No." Reaching out, I stopped her from moving further into the darkness. I pulled her in, though she struggled against my hold. "Are you crazy?"

"But I want to see!"

"It's too dark to see!" I hissed in her ear. "And dangerous. Any sort of animal could be living down here, and this tunnel probably hasn't been used in years."

As I said the words, something twisted hard in my stomach. I didn't like it, and I wanted nothing more than to just get out of here. I tugged her arm again, starting to head toward the hole we had dug. "Come on. It's not safe down here. We should go."

It was only once I finished talking, in the pause before she could wrangle up a response, that I heard it. She must have heard it, too, her body stiffening next to me and her shoulder brushing mine in the effort to get closer. It was the sound of something dragging wetly, like a mop, across the dirt floor, followed by a slow, low moaning.

It was a sound we'd both heard before, little more than a year ago. A sound we both thought we'd never hear again.

She whispered my name, whimpering, reaching for my hand. In what little light we had from the hole, I could see that her eyes were wide, gleaming, like she was about to start crying.

"Shhh." I swallowed hard as another soft moan seemed to rise up from the walls of the tunnel. "It's okay. We'll just move slowly, back to the entrance, crawl back out."

"They'll see us!"

"No, they won't. Not if we're slow and careful and silent." I tried to nudge her behind me. "Go first."

"They'll hear us!" she hissed, the harshness of it making me wince. I struggled to keep my own voice low and quiet and calm.

"No, they won't. We just have to be careful…"

"We'll never make it out in time!"

"Yes, we will."

"I thought they all died!"

Her voice had reached a pitch that made me sure that this was the end. The shuffling sound stopped; they were orientating themselves, readjusting their focus. I heard another low groan and realized that it came from me this time.

She was in hysterics. "They all died! They all stopped! They couldn't survive the winters! Why, God, why…"

"Spring thaw," I realized, despondency freezing me in place. "The spring thaw, and they were still down here, after all these years."

Her scream pulled me out of my head, loud and terrified in my ear, and I felt the cold, slimy brush of decaying flesh against my arm. "No!" I shouted, snapping back into the terrible reality around us. I pulled back my fist and shot it forward, the knuckles connecting with something soft and hard all at once. My other hand reached for her. I wrenched her arm away from a cold grip. She was still screaming bloody murder, drawing more of them toward us, and I all but shoved her into the tunnel's open. "Go!"

"We'll never make it!" she cried.

"Not if you don't go!"

"They're all supposed to be dead!" Her wail was so desperate that despair almost rendered me motionless again. That terrified sob held all the memories of when they first showed up, all those years ago, before the winters froze them and we thought we had gotten rid of them for good. But we hadn't. And that's what kept me going.

"God damn it, go!" I gave her a push so strong that she could do little more than cry out as if injured, as if I was doing something worse to her than what they might do. She crawled awkwardly forward, and I kept pushing, freeing enough room for me to start to crawl up behind her. I kept pushing, pushing, pushing. She sobbed in contempt, in terror, but she kept moving. Every time something behind us moaned, she'd almost buckle again. But we had to keep pushing.

Just as I could see the end of the tunnel, the light breaking around her form, I felt a tug, surprisingly strong, on my leg. It was strong enough that I fell, chest and face smashing into the dirt. It pulled again, sharper this time. I dug my fingernails into the ground, clinging with conviction. But they were so strong. I gnashed my teeth together, straining against their hungry, dogged pulls.

She was out of the hole now, shouting my name, but, realizing my struggle, she came back to try to pull me out with her. Her fingers had only just barely brushed mine before a firm pull rendered me out of her reach.

"No!" I told her quickly. "Leave me! Get yourself out! Go warn everyone that they're still here."

"No." Her face was a mask of tears, her voice a terrified, shaking tremble. "I can't leave you."

She tried to reach for me again. The moans behind me grew, and I felt more hands at my ankles. Futilely, I kicked.

"Damn it!" I growled. "Go! You're not stronger than them! They'll get us both!"

"I can't!"

"God damn it!"

Kicking seemed to dislodge them, but only temporarily. She hovered at the entrance, blubbering and shuddering with indecision.

"This is all my fault!" she moaned.

"Get out of here!"

It was all her fault; I couldn't deny that. If she hadn't insisted on digging, I wouldn't be here, under the earth, clinging to dirt for my life. But we were here, and there was only one thing we could do about it.

"God damn it," I growled, "they'll kill us both if you don't move your stupid ass and get out of here!"

Another yank. I moved back another few inches before I was able to stop myself. A low moan left me as I felt their teeth starting to nibble at my calf. Weakness overwhelmed me; my vision was starting to sway, and all the words in my repertoire abandoned me, leaving only pained howls.

It's difficult to remember much after that. There was a sharp scream, but I think it came from somewhere inside of myself, not from her. I was pulled back again, roughly and completely. She was receding from my vision, finally, and though I told her to go, I found myself reaching out for her desperately. The darkness surrounded me as did the sounds of all their horrible moaning, their clammy hands pawed all over my body. So many hands, cold and damp and dirty, reaching and clawing and grabbing, ripping my shirt, rending my flesh.

Warm, wet mouths with sharp teeth sank into my sides, my legs, my shoulder, sucking all my blood and sinew. I felt lightheaded. I could hear myself crying even over the sounds of their grateful murmurs and ceaseless gnawing.

Then they stopped.

Everything stopped.

All I can remember now is how I got here, my insatiable hunger, and how, in the first early days of spring, when the world slowly warmed by the lazy heat of a pale sun and the trees were budding with the yellow-green promise of things to come, we'll slowly warm and live again.

Kanoa

When she was flying, Kanoa was free. The sky, unlike the earth, could not hold her down. She could go anywhere, soaring over the world below with a steady beat of her wings and the rush of the warm breeze through her feathers. If she could wish for anything in the entire world, it would be for boundless energy, so she would never have to stop and rest, she could just fly from one edge of the sky to the other.

Kanoa knew the whole island from her bird's eye view, from the bright white sands of the northern edge, where all the tourists with their pale flesh and bright bathing suits flocked. There was their humble but sprawling town, with its center littered with taller buildings all encased in glass that blinded her when the sun caught them in just the right way. The rolling hills with their thick jungles, building up into the mountains, too hard for so many trees, and then the volcano, its blasted top dark and foreboding, silent now, but there was always the feeling of danger looming over it. And, as the land sloped back down on the other side, there was the place they called the Barren Lands, all dark rocks and sturdy plants, mysterious coves of water and gloomy, unexplored caverns. She loved her island, and this view of it, shared only with other birds and the occasional helicopter with its thumping propellers.

As the sky started to darken, though, Kanoa would have to descend. She always lingered until the red or purples or oranges of the beautiful sunsets faded away into grey. One of these nights, she vowed she would take a flight through the blanket of pin-pointed stars, through misty grey clouds, right toward the full pale moon. That night, unfortunately, was far away, and, as evening settled in, she realized she was already late, and she was already in trouble.

Landing softly in the field of grass not far from their home, Kanoa silently lamented the loss of her wings. Slowly, she felt her human body returning to her; after each transformation, she wished she would never have to return to this form, bound by so much, that she could remain a bird forever. After the grace given by a flight, her long limbs felt ungainly and awkward. Her bones felt heavy and her skin seemed to be in a constant state of gooseflesh, cold from the lack of insulating, comforting feathers.

And then there was everything else that went with being human. Responsibility, relatives, the reality of gravity. Kanoa shuddered a little as she jogged down the street toward her house, dreading the moment she walked through that door. Maybe, she thought, hoping against hope, there would be no one there. Maybe her sister went out with her friends. Her uncle had gone out on a job or drinking with his buddies. Her aunt was at some random midnight mass for some random made-up sounding saint.

The windows were bright with light, though, and Kanoa braced herself for the usual onslaught of disappointment from her family. She slipped around toward the back of building; in his cage, Ilio shifted, standing bolt upright, but he did not bark. Kanoa only saw the dark shadow of his tail whipping from side to side, possibly the only one happy to see her. It made her smile, though only briefly, wondering why she didn't just stay out there with the dog. He would have made much more pleasant company. But she went ahead, steeled herself as she pushed open the door and tiptoed as quietly as she could into the kitchen.

Kanoa made it about three steps before there was a hand on her arm, tight as a vice. "Where have you been?" Makana hissed, pulling her younger sister closer. Her voice was quiet, whispered, not wanting to attract attention from the other room, where the sounds of canned laughter poured from the television.

Trying not to whimper, trying not to squirm, Kanoa glowered at Makana. "I was out running naked in the volcano for Pele," she muttered, knowing the sarcasm would earn her a burning twist on her arm.

"You were flying again," Makana accused. "How stupid are you?"

"Let me go!" She gave into the squirming, trying to pull her arm away from her sister's grip.

When that didn't work, she realized she had to try a little harder, reaching out to grab Makana, push her back. Makana tugged her arm down sharply, making her shout out with the pain, and then they both winced. There was no way their scuffle would go unnoticed.

"Oh, my Lord." Aunt Lani stood now in the kitchen door, swathed in her fluffy pink robe and the matching slippers. As usual, her head was festooned with a crown of rollers. So much for her being at a church meeting; she looked more like Medusa than a God-fearing woman. "You nuggets are going to drive me right up this wall. You know your uncle isn't going to like the two of you fighting like rabid dogs in here."

Almost as if on cue, Uncle Jon's voice drifted through from the living room, rising over the soundtrack of whatever he was watching. "You tell those girls that if they don't shut up in there, I will shut them up myself."

For a moment, Kanoa thought Makana might give her away. Her sister's chest swelled up with a deep breath, her jaw set tightly as she weighed the choices, and Kanoa realized that she wasn't breathing either. She tried not to look at Makana too much, but she knew her fate was in her sister's hands. She closed her eyes, tried to think of flying, though perhaps that was the wrong way to go. Makana did not have the same powers as Kanoa, and it had always been a point of contention with her.

"We're sorry, Aunt Lani," Makana finally spoke quietly. "I was just getting Kanoa inside. She was out playing with Ilio and lost track of the time."

Aunt Lani's bleary, watery eyes narrowed in suspicion, but Kanoa made a fine show out of keeping her face blank. It helped to transport herself to a few short moments ago, when she could still feel the wind on her face. "All right, then," she said, reluctantly. "You girls get on up to bed, and stop making all this noise. Your uncle had a bad day, and the least you could do is keep it quiet and be civil instead of acting like savages. It's hard enough for us to take care of you since your parents went and died like they did, you know."

"Yes, ma'am," the two of them muttered, in unison, as they had been doing for nearly a decade of living under this roof. They kept their eyes down and their hands folded and, after Aunt Lani sent them one more warning glare, they scurried toward the stairs up to their small attic bedroom. Makana had grabbed Kanoa's hand, practically dragging her on the way, and when they reached their room, she turned on her vehemence.

"You really are stupid, you know that?" she said, shaking her head and sulking toward her bed, plopping down on it. "If they knew you'd been going out to turn into a bird and flying, Kanoa, that'll be the end of it! Did you know Uncle Jon's been talking about sending us off? We're so close; one more year, and I'll be eighteen, and we can be out of this house, but not if you go screwing it up by doing that."

"I'm sorry!" It came out of Kanoa with more desperation than she'd intended. "I can't help it! You don't understand!"

"I know," Makana said, after a moment, giving Kanoa a faint smile. "I don't, but I understand it a whole lot more than they will. Come on. I'm going to bed. You know Aunt Lani's going to want us up early tomorrow for church."

Feeling numb, Kanoa went through the motions of getting ready with her sister, who offered a hug, reminded her that she loved her and that, if she could keep it together and keep from transforming, then their parents would look down on them and be proud of her. But Kanoa knew that she couldn't. She had to fly. She lay still in her bed for the longest time, wondering if she could get through another year of this. This house seemed so small and restrictive, her aunt and uncle so cruel and always holding it against them that they were a burden, and Makana had changed so much from when they were little girls together. She waited until she heard the soft, slow breathing of Makana's sleep before slipping out of her bed, slipping toward the window, and opening it as quietly as she could.

The night sky was sprinkled with stars, as wide and fathomless as the blue from earlier. Down below, Ilio was watching from his cage, his tail wagging back and forth as if to invite her out.

Kanoa closed her eyes and pushed off the window ledge, flapping her wings and heading for the moon.

Bibliophile

With shaking hands, Christian ran his fingers over the rough surface of the book's cover. The leather was so old, but the years had been kind to it. His left hand caressed its broken spine; his right hand pressed against the ragged pages of the fore edge. He brought it directly under his nose and took a deep breath. Forget that fabled scent of a woman to create a dizzying intoxication. These musty pages were more potent than any drug, these books more apt a lover than any girl could ever be. He couldn't imagine a more beguiling mistress.

And this one…oh, this one was a particularly exquisite discovery. After a moment of appreciation, Christian opened his eyes, glancing around suspiciously. Could Vaja really be oblivious to this precious jewel just lying there, disregarded, among so many mundane volumes on these broken, battered bookshelves? For the tenth time in the few minutes since finding it, he checked the inside cover, which creaked slightly as it was pulled away from the other pages. And, for the tenth time, he was assured that it was authentic, thanks to three unmistakable marks: the author's ink-printed sigil, the written authority of the royal publishers, and the pressed mark of the Great Freeland Library. It was even in the original Kyanese. No forger would ever go through that much trouble.

Christian's heart began to race again. He held the book tightly to his chest as if to silence the quickening thumps.

Vaja was busy with another customer, a bright-eyed young woman who talked vividly with laughs and gestures. This kept the storekeeper distracted enough that he wouldn't notice Christian staring, brow furrowed in thought. He was intently considering what might happen when he approached the flimsy, fold-out table at the front of the store to make his purchase. Would Vaja recognize the treasure immediately, giving Christian a harder time and a higher price? Or would it slip entirely under his radar? After all, it seemed to have gone unnoticed when it was put on the shelf. It was impossible for him to have overlooked its value then, if he realized it at all. What if he did know, though, and had left it there for Christian to find? No. That was too far-fetched. Christian wasn't the only one that came to this little hovel for the occasional rare find. Anyone could have noticed it and swiped it up; Vaja wouldn't have taken that risk.

Just to be safe, Christian reached over and grabbed a stack of random books to his left, tucking them under his arm after slipping his prize in between them. He tried to seem nonchalant as he wandered toward Vaja. He examined the books purchased by the girl just before they were shoved into a plastic bag and handed over to their new owner. They were some religious books, most of them quite old, and one recently published fiction from Midacia. Christian had heard of it, but hadn't read it. The girl thanked Vaja and regarded Christian with a bright smile. He returned it weakly, nodding his head in approval of her selections. She danced out the door, and Christian, trying to ignore his nervous apprehensions, took her place at the table.

"Are we having...feminine problems, Chris?" Vaja arched an eyebrow as he peered inside the cover of the first book, refusing to lift his eyes as he jotted down the price and unfortunate title: *What's Happening to Me? A Young Woman's Guide to Cramps, Bloating, Migraines and Other Menstrual Woes.*

Throat constricting and an immediate blush filling his pale cheeks, Christian was surprisingly quick with an excuse, though he wished he'd taken more care in selecting his random books. "You never know when that sort of information might be useful." Working up a bit of passionate flare, he tapped a finger pointedly on the table. "That book was written by a government scientist. Who knows how fraudulent some of that information is compared to other sources? Someone has to make sure that they aren't corrupting our youth with unprecedented ideas."

Vaja maintained a doubtful look.

Christian rolled his eyes and sighed. "Well, you didn't have any books on male puberty, so what does that say about you?"

Vaja snorted a semblance of a laugh and continued on through the stack, scribbling away fluidly and without any further comment. It wasn't long before there was only one book before Christian's prize. He couldn't help holding his breath. Vaja looked up at Christian expectantly, and he spoke.

Christian was both started and confused, the words that came out of Vaja's mouth lost in his nervousness. "I'm sorry?" The question staggered out of him, frowning, dreading what had been said.

"I said, I see you've found her." A smile slipped onto Vaja's dark, wrinkled face. It forced his eyes mostly closed, but Christian could still see the mischievous sparkle in them.

Christian was astounded. So Vaja did leave it there for him to find. He felt a great surge of appreciation and happiness, though it was quickly replaced with a sharp anger.

"What were you thinking, you old coot?" He was yelling, but after a glance around the store, he lowered his voice. He brought his face down close to the grinning shopkeeper. "Leaving something this incredibly valuable just out there for anyone to see? Have you finally lost your mind?"

Vaja bristled slightly, his lips puckering as if he'd tasted a lemon. "Oh, get off it, Christian," he mumbled, rolling his eyes. "How many people do you think come in here and realize the value of an old book like that? Besides, I just set it out before you showed up. You work on a very particular schedule, you know. I'd kept it in the back until today. I just wanted to see how you'd react to finding it here." He started chuckling. "Never imagined you'd resort to teen health books."

Before the words were even out of Vaja's mouth, the deep blush had returned to Christian's cheeks, replacing the brief flare of anger. "Yeah, well...uh..." Sighing heavily, he shook his head, giving up. "Just total them up, will you?"

The chuckling developed into a full-fledged belly laugh, drawing, again, a few curious eyes. Christian lowered his head. "Don't feel like you still have to buy them, Chris."

Christian brushed a strand of his hair behind his ear. "Thanks, Vaja," he said. "But go ahead and keep that one by Averok. And the physics one. And...aw, damn, I'll take all of them anyway. I meant it as an excuse, but I think there might actually be something in that theory about the government scientists corrupting our pubescent young girls. And one can never have too many books."

"Keep that philosophy," Vaja said, stuffing the books into a bag, "and I'll be able to keep my family fed."

Money was exchanged, pulled from the recesses of a weathered leather wallet, and Christian held his new purchases close to his chest as he stepped out of the dusty shop, into the grimy streets of Analisia City. The smell beyond the door of Vaja's hovel was not nearly as wonderful; he always almost gagged at the sudden transition from musty literature to fuel emissions and piss. Daylight weakly forced its way through the thickly hanging clouds overhead, giving everything a strange, faded appearance, like the old photographs he sometimes found tucked away in used books, the edges yellow with a disease that would soon creep over the entire image. Only, those photographs were quaint, depicting a world that had long since been buried under the glistening facade of progress, quickly deteriorating into the slums of disenchantment. He frowned, turning his eyes up toward where the government center jutted out over the dividing highway, roaring with complaints of too many vehicles. Did people truly wonder why he preferred books to this?

He started down the streets, toward the rows of brownstone buildings that used to be red, toward the narrow stairwell that he'd take into his dark apartment. When he got there, he would saunter immediately toward the drafting table in the northwest corner, switching on the light that would flood the flawless white surface. He would slip on a pair of immaculate latex gloves, snapping them against his wrists as he flexed and pulled for a good fit. Carefully, tenderly, gently, he would remove the book from the bag and place it delicately on the table. Like a skilled doctor about to perform a crucial surgery, he would slip into the dissection of the words, cutting them apart as he scribbled notes in a small notepad, consulting one of his tattered, archaic language dictionaries. Like the complicated locks on an Analisian puzzle box, he'd slowly discover the wonderful voice of the book's author, a rich message that would seem written specifically for him.

Christian sighed wistfully, forgetting for a moment that he wasn't actually there yet. Someone had sidled up beside him, though. He knew better than to acknowledge that he had seen them, but he kept the figure at the back of his mind and paid more attention to the pockets of his jeans. It could be anyone. A mugger, a street urchin, a hooker. None of whom seemed someone who'd want anything to do with him. His shirt was dirty and his hair unwashed, so he couldn't possibly project an aura of having any money. He did have shoes, though. He held his books tighter, so he muscles would flex, and he kept walking as if no one was there.

He didn't have to pretend for too long. They were barely past the sharp, spicy smells of Alibin's Kassirian Restaurant before the ghost at his side started to giggle, girlish and free, a bubbling that tumbled into a laugh. It was such a random, peculiar response that Christian couldn't help but acknowledge it.

"What?" he demanded gruffly. He instantly felt bad about it when he saw that his shadow was actually a pretty girl.

Very pretty, wide-eyed with long dark hair, a red beret perched on her head. He recognized her as the girl from the bookshop. "I'm sorry," she said through a light smile. "I guess you won."

What a peculiar thing to say. Christian ruminated over it, but didn't respond.

"So," she continued, "you're the man Vaja was holding that book for."

Christian flinched. He knew Vaja was being stupid by having it lying out for anyone to notice, but at least he hadn't let her buy it. That she had tried increased his desire to associate with her, even if she did end a sentence in a preposition. "Are you a fan of Allok's work?" he asked. It was a stupid question, really. If she was, she would have fought harder for the book.

"Not particularly," she said, as he had expected. "I just like old books."

Christian grunted, severely unsatisfied. Of course she did. Probably made her feel smart.

He felt her eyes dancing over him. Was she searching for a new topic? Why? If she wanted his attention, she should start quoting Cohl or maybe some Locin. Then she could start impressing him. But no one quoted Cohl or Locin anymore.

"I noticed," she started up again, "that the book was in Kyanese. Not many people speak Kyanese. Do you?"

Was that admiration glistening in her eyes? No. No one spoke Kyanese anymore because no one cared, so why should she? "No," he said softly. "I just translate it."

"Oh, is that what you do, then? For a living?"

His eyes narrowed slightly as he slid them toward her, examining her expression. Faint smile, glistening eyes. Genuine interest. But why? The conversation so far suggested that it wasn't the material that captivated her, so, logically, it had to be him, but that was even more puzzling. It was possible that she was scouting him. Figure out what a man did for a living and a girl could effectively map out an eventual future, particularly if the man made a lot of money.

His gaze lingered for a moment toward her chest, to see if taking that chance was worth it, but her collared shirt-and-sweater combination didn't reveal much. He sighed. "No. Well, sometimes, but it's more of a hobby than a profession."

"Well, what do you do for a living, then?"

So she was that type of girl. Or maybe not. When Christian looked toward her again, there was something about her that seemed completely sincere. He considered, for a moment, her crisp black skirt, that fuzzy sweater, her red beret. "Do you often just pick random strangers from the streets and ask them personal questions?" he asked.

She blinked at him, looking puzzled.

"You're new here in the city, aren't you?"

She smiled then, looking down, a deeply bashful expression. "I just moved here last week."

"And you're probably from one of those small towns up north, like Balfor or Hijan, or something."

She laughed; it was a strange sound to him. Too light, too carefree. It made him feel uncomfortable. "Further north, actually. I'm from Kyano, a small place you've probably never heard of."

Another preposition. "Kyano? Is that why you...?"

"Recognized the language? Yeah. I didn't want to mention anything because, well, I didn't want you to know that I wasn't from around here." She laughed again; her hand was suddenly on his arm. Christian tried not to pull away. "Pretty silly, huh? I still can't understand it, though. I don't even think my grandpop knows that old language stuff."

A foreigner. That explained why she was so unassuming and friendly. Christian frowned, pondering this new information. Maybe if he scowled hard enough, she'd get timid and afraid, influenced by all the stories about the scary city, and leave him alone. Girls were so difficult to comprehend. Why couldn't they be more like books? With books, it was all there, laid out for you. Sometimes you had to search the spaces between the lines to fully understand, but, with women, you constantly had to consider what existed in unspoken subtext. It frustrated him.

"So what's your name?"

He sighed. "Christian."

"I'm Jack." She grinned wildly. "Wanna go get some caulfae?"

"That's an odd name for a girl."

"I think it's kind of cute. Come on! How about it? There's that cute shop right on the other side of the by-way; I pass it every day, and I've wanted to step in, but I'm so silly and bashful about new places when I'm by myself."

This bothered Christian immensely, his frown growing deeper and genuine. Too silly and bashful to enter a caulfae shop, but she had no problem coming up to and bothering a complete stranger in the street? "Listen, Jack," he finally said, stopping to turn and look at her so she would comprehend the dire seriousness in his voice. "You're a really sweet girl and I appreciate your offer, but I really just want to get back to my apartment and start going through these books. It's nothing against you or anything like that. I just want to get to work."

"Oh, please come?" She said it with the sounds all smushed like oatmeal. Her thin hands wrapped around his wrist softly.

Sharply, he pulled his arm away. The touch frightened him, but not nearly as much as the feeling that raced through him. It was like a shock, those little fingers around his tiny wrist, like the snap of his gloves. He considered just breaking out into a run, a frantic dash toward the safety of his apartment. But…

Why couldn't he just refuse this girl? He didn't want anything to do with her anymore; she was starting to make him feel so strange and uncomfortable. Perhaps it was something to do with estrogen. Perhaps he'd have to break open that puberty book when he got home and find some answer about the mysterious nature of the feminine species there.

Christian arched an eyebrow at her expectantly.

Jack smiled, a soft grin that developed with a sigh of relief. She even placed one of her hands to her chest; Christian could only assume she was calming a feverish heart. "How about another time, then? Tomorrow, maybe three in the afternoon? You'll have plenty of time to pour over those pages by then, right?"

Barely. But he said, "Okay."

Black Stones

He was building the bridge stone by stone. George stopped and straightened, stretching out his aching back and brushing the damp hair out of his eyes. The island, as well as the sentinel of a castle perched upon it, seemed close enough that he could almost reach out and touch it, open his hand and close his fingers around it, bringing it in, close to his heart. But he could only look across the channel that separated him from the island wistfully. He sighed, reaching into the wheelbarrow for another rock and dropping it lazily at his feet. It clattered against the others, rolled into the water without as much as a splash.

"That's the last of them," he announced, brushing his hands against each other, then against the salty stiffness of his pants. His eyes fell, despondent, into the empty barrow, across the rocks they had dropped so far, and to the wide gap left between where the stones ended and the island began. It pained him to say these next words. "We'll have to call it a day."

"This is ridiculous," said his friend, surly and sour with his stooped shoulders and scowling face. "We're never going to make it across this way, not until we're old men, bent and crippled. And by then, your princess won't even want you, George, and you may not want your princess."

Despite the harsh words, George gave his friend a small, faint smile. "I will always want my princess. And she will always want me. This must be done, Roderick. Black stones to lead the way and, once I am across, the great waters will take the stones with them, and she and I will be safe in our stronghold until the end of time."

Roderick shook his head, turning away, ready to be finished with the work and his friend's lunatic ravings. Everyone knew the castle was empty, had been for centuries, and yet, as Roderick drifted away and the sun turned red with the bleeding of the setting sun, George lingered, staring at the highest pulpit of the tower. It was shrouded in shadows, but George liked to think that, if he looked closely, he could see a flash of a white handkerchief. The princess waving to him, surrendering to her hope that, one day, the bridge of black stones would be complete, and they would be together.

Feeling the swell of his heart in his chest, George lifted his hand in acknowledgement to his mysterious princess, and he stayed for a good long moment, as if expecting the exchange to continue. But the castle stood, cold and black, and the warmth of the day was quickly descending into a chill as the sun disappeared. He turned and followed after Roderick, steeling himself to not look back. He did, though, just before disappearing through the forest path, one last glance so the princess would know his silent vow to return again, every day, until the bridge was built.

The next day, he went to the field to collect the stones in the trusted wheelbarrow without Roderick. The process was much slower. With the two of them, the barrow could be filled of the black stones within an hour. This would take closer to two, and he might upset the others with his tardiness, but if he loaded the barrow now, returned to what was expected of him, then he would have a chance to unload the stones by afternoon, return to reload, and do twice as much work in the entire day with a second trip. So, at the break of dawn, while traces of night still hung in the lavender sky, he slipped out of the quiet house and down to the field to start gathering his stones.

He must have lost track of the time, though, because George looked up from dropping another stone into the barrow to see two figures not far away at the fence bordering the field. His sister was sitting there, perched up on the fence with their younger brother at her feet. The wind whipped Catherine's long curtain of red hair across her face, and she patiently tucked it behind her ear again, so as not to interrupt the steady, unwavering look locked onto George. Young Peter extracted the thumb out of his mouth and lifted his hand in a lazy little wave.

He considered saying something to them, but shook his head and went back to work, wondering how long they had been there. Eventually, Catherine spoke, just as he expected she would. "Mother wants you to come home,

George," she stated, her voice lifting slightly to carry across the distance between them. "She says if we do not fetch you now, then you will spend all day at this ridiculous nonsense."

George realized he could have explained that it was not nonsense at all and that he had no intention of ceasing, but he decided to let his actions speak for him instead. Speaking would waste energy, potentially sparking an argument. He would brook no argument on this. There was too much work to do.

But Catherine didn't say anything more, either. She just sat there, watching, until George felt a nervousness creep up his spine. Noticing that the wheelbarrow was still not nearly as full as he had hoped, he dropped a black stone into it, released a sigh from exertion with his hands on his hips, and glowered at the scrawny girl. "I don't suppose you could lend a helping hand," he stated pointedly.

"I will have no hand in supporting your insanity," remarked Catherine with just as much aplomb. "Mother says come home now, George."

"The sooner I load this barrow, Catherine," he responded, "the sooner I will come home. Help me, and I shall finish sooner."

Catherine slid off the fence and reached her hand down to take Peter's. "This is not good, George," she said. "It was a strange fancy at first, but now, this chasing of a tale told to babes is going to wreak dangerous consequences. Come,

Peter." With a small tug, she pulled the little one into movement, but those wide, deep eyes lingered on George for a long while. Though there was more work to be done, he waited until they had disappeared down the path through the trees before continuing, and he continued on until well after the midday hour.

He did return home after that, to help with the chores, to have his mother look at him with her eyes wide and haunted and confused. Knowing what his response would be, she asked what he intended on doing when he was finished, and he wilted under the disapproval that surfaced when he told her, not wanting to lie. He knew it hurt his mother to see him so possessed with this task, but surely she must understand its importance. He thought he saw Catherine narrow her eyes, glowering at him from across the room, but he ignored it, turning his mind to ways to speed up the bridge building while his hands worked mindlessly at his other tasks, which seemed so useless and insignificant in comparison.

It was late when he finally shuffled back to his bed, under what little starlight remained. And dawn had only just started to emerge when he was back in the field again, finding more rocks. Collecting and building, building and collecting. It felt as though he was getting closer and closer across the dark, treacherous water between him and the castle when he left, but when he arrived for work the next day, he seemed further away than ever before.

It went on like that for several days, and, every so often, Roderick would join him, or Catherine would sit on the fence and watch. Sometimes, she had Peter with her, but she never helped. She just stared, occasionally throwing out the usual warnings and reprimands on how he should stop. Then came the day when the wind was so strong, it not only blew her hair into her face, but seemed to threaten to sweep her off her feet entirely. She didn't sit on the fence that day, but clung onto it with both hands, lifting her voice in a shout to be carried to his ears on the stiff winds.

"George!" she called. "You have to come back home! There's a storm in the air; they say it already hit down in Monarch's Glen. Please, George, come home! It would be madness to go out to the castle today!"

Roderick was with her, though he hadn't noticed him there until he had put his hand on Catherine's arm and tried to pull her away. "Come," he said. "Leave him to his madness. We should get you safe."

George considered doing as he always did, not even bothering to grace her with a response, but he thought of the castle, the tall dark shape looming over the rushing waters, the bridge of black stones almost complete, and the flash of a waving white handkerchief in the darkened windows, and he shook his head. "I can't," he said. "I'm so close,

Catherine. I can't give up. Go with Roderick! I must do this."

"George." Even with the howling wind, the heartbreak in her words could be heard, her face disappearing in a cloud of red hair one moment, and then illuminated as lightning ripped through the sky. "Please."

"This is madness, George!" Roderick chimed in, turning worried eyes toward the sky and the approaching rain.

Knowing there was nothing any of them could say to move the other, George just continued working, turning his back on his sister and his friend. He continued to lift the rocks from the field, into the wheelbarrow; they were becoming harder and harder to find in the long grass; it had taken him all day to fill it, but this was the night, this was the day he would finally complete the bridge to the castle. He would just keep looking a little longer, fill it up a little more. Eventually, Catherine had given up, or perhaps merely given in to Roderick's will and gentle goading, and they drifted away like ghosts. The rain started to fall on his cheeks in fat, wet drops, the sky darkening quickly with the cover of menacing clouds and the unforgiving nighttime.

The wind whipped at his back as he trudged forward, his hands cold as they gripped the slickening handles of the wheelbarrow, pushing forward through the storm, through the forest path, down to the straight and the island with the castle looming like an immovable mountain in the quickening darkness. He put his head down and hurried forward, fighting against the great gusts that pushed the water up over the bridge he had been building. A flash of light streaked across the sky, sending everything into a sharp contrast before descending back into black again with a low rumble. His feet slid on the rocks as he angled his barrow toward them, and the gushing wind was strong enough to nearly push him over. He kept moving, though, until he reached the end of the bridge, the water drenching his boots, his trousers, his hair clinging to his face and practically blinding him.

But he didn't need to see to know what he was to do. He could lift the stones and drop them blindly, and he did, working despite the fact that the rain and wind were now becoming whips, and he could feel every wet lash through his muscles. Still he worked, straining against the pain, ignoring the figures that appeared at the shore, at the start of the bridge, cloaks and hair whipping about them as they shouted out to him. The wind howled, taking their words with it, so that he couldn't hear them begging for him to come back. Roderick, and his sister, shouting about the storm, shouting about his safety, his sanity. His fingers wrapped around another black stone, lifting it up, setting it down. And then he picked up another stone, set it down. Another and another, until all he knew was his fatigue and his fingers scraping into the bottom of the barrow, filled with rain water, and there were no more black stones.

In the morning, after the storm, there was also no George. The only sign that he had been there was the overturned wheelbarrow set a few paces from the shore; even the long line of black stones had been completely washed away with the wind and the rain and the storm. All that remained between the island and the shore was the dark, turbulent waters. No one would give a voice to their thoughts, averting their eyes and shuffling by with uncomfortable acceptance. No one dared to speak of what the storm had likely done to the poor madman.

Catherine slipped away that morning, with Peter trailing behind her, always trailing, and they went to the shore where the castle loomed, black and still and immovable, on the other side of the straight. Tightening her fist, Catherine quietly cursed the castle, cursed the rain, cursed the black stones that had washed away. And, beside her, quietly looking up, Peter thought he saw the faint glimmer of something in the tower's highest window. A flash of candlelight, or perhaps a white handkerchief. He shyly lifted his hand and waved, and he would swear he saw someone waving back.

Purgatory

Quietly, she opens the door and slips into the room, bare toes on the hardwood floor. They're painted bubblegum pink. The door creaks as she passes, causing her to wince and glance worriedly toward the bed. But he doesn't wake, doesn't stir. The only movement is the cat's curious head lifting from where he's curled up. He uncoils to spread out his long, limber body. He doesn't meow, doesn't give her away. He just yawns, settling in a new position where he watches her plaintively as she strips off her and slips in quietly between the cool cotton sheets.

The cat waits patiently for her to settle in before curling up again, this time between them to soak up the warmth from their two bodies.

In the morning: "Did I wake you?"

She should just keep her mouth shut, but she asks anyway, perhaps out of guilt, perhaps to simply acknowledge her tardiness and move on with it.

He yawns, clinging to his empty coffee cup with one hand while the other scratches at his crotch. His mouth stretches to its peak, before he attempts to mumble something. He reaches for the coffee pot and tries to annunciate better. "What time'd you get in?"

"Don't know," she says. "I wasn't really paying attention."

But she had been. It was 2:27, red numbers glaring through the darkness. She finds herself yawning now, but she, unlike him, unlike the cat, she discretely hides it behind her hand. She flips the eggs. "Thank God it's Saturday."

"We should have slept in more," he says, somehow finding a mischievous smile. "We deserve it."

She snorts, glad for the genuine smirk that surfaces. "If we slept in, we'd get nothing done today."

"You planned on get anything done today?" His tone is playful, and she laughs, noting how it actually feels natural. She starts to feel a little twist of guilt for her late night excursions under the guise of work, but she also feels a spark of hope that maybe things aren't so bad between them after all.

"I was going to at least try!"

"Only one thing I want to do today."

"Oh yeah?" she asks, and, suddenly, that quickly, everything shifts. She feels a pit harden in her stomach, but she maintains her smile. "What's that?"

And, as she expects, as she fears, he reaches over to grab her hand. The kitchen is small enough that he does so easily, and he pulls her in, like reeling in a fish. One arm sliding around her waist, he draws her in for a kiss. It's a long, slow kiss, giving her plenty of time to squirm. He has to know that she doesn't want it, doesn't he? She considers humoring him, but she can't. She just can't.

"The eggs," she tells him, when she can finally come up for air. Her escape card, her get-out-of-jail-free pass. "They'll burn."

"Let them." He looks up at her pleadingly. It almost gets her, those soulful grey eyes with just a hint of reproach.

"I can't," she says apologetically. But she does lean down to kiss his forehead, as if that could be an appropriate consolation prize. He lets her go; he knows she means it. They've reached a point in their lives where the fiscal responsibility of never wasting perfectly good food trumps sexual desire.

Everything trumps sexual desire these days. Between each other, anyway.

Eggs. Bacon. Pancakes. For everything that's changed between them, Saturday breakfasts remain the same. The conversations have all but halted, replaced with forks against plates, the slight crunch of crispy bacon. He likes it crispy; she does not. Sometimes, she'll make it less crispy on purpose. But not today. Today, it snaps like twigs, and she complains about it being burnt, and he reassures her that it's really good, it's perfect, which only makes her doubt it more.

"You've been working too hard," he says, later, drying as she washes the dishes.

"I know." She warily looks over at him, marveling at how easy it was to look him straight in the eye and lie right to his face. "But we need it."

"I know," he says, just as quietly, and then they're silent again, nothing but running water and closing cupboards.

"I've been looking for new work," he offers, eventually, a bit too conversationally. "Late shifts. We can be on the same schedule."

She doesn't like how that causes her heart to flutter against her chest, but she knows she deserves it. There is no new work out there; she's looked for it herself. But she uses that excuse, too. She knows what it means. The same schedule. When together, together. When apart... far apart.

She wants to cry, but she knows that isn't fair. Maybe she should have let him kiss her earlier, but she knows she couldn't stand it. She turns off the faucet.

"You'll find something," she says. "I know you will."

He smiles back at her, so innocent that she thinks maybe she's wrong, but, when he moves, he kisses her on the cheek and the thoughts return. "Bathroom," he announces and disappears up the stairs. She is left standing in the kitchen, dishcloth absently rubbing the water from her hands, drying them.

That leaves just her and the cat. She looks at him, and he returns the simple gaze. Blinks his eyes and asks an unsaid question. He alone seems privy to the secrets between them, and then he stretches, like he had last night, long and languid. He pads calmly out of the kitchen, and then it's just her.

The Space Between Worlds

The hand on the clock moved, shuddering, clicking into place. The music of the bells rang out over the courtyard, announcing to the world the late afternoon hour. As the soft breeze carried the music into her bedroom, stirring the curtain, Emalia opened her eyes. Though the warm sun spilled in through the open window, she gasped as if she had been struck by a sudden and terrible chill. For a moment, she wasn't even sure where she was, but the details slowly started to fall into place. The soft feather mattress, the crisp linen sheets, the birds chirping sing-song in the flowering apple tree right outside. Her bedroom. Springtime. She turned her head to the side and, sure enough, rocking steadily in her chair with a ball of bright yellow yarn quickly being knitted into shape, was her Aunt Marie-Claire, smiling softly at her.

"And there you are, ma petit!" she said with her bubbling, happy voice. The needles in her hand kept clicking steadily, perfectly timed with the ticking of the small clock on top of the chest of drawers. Once the last bell had faded in the courtyard, the passing seconds seemed to invade the warm, cozy room. "Welcome back. How was your little journey this time?"

Emalia frowned, opening her mouth to answer, but she found it too dry. She worked her tongue and her lips a bit while she slowly sat up, pushing herself up on her elbows. Her head was pounding, and the world seemed to tilt a little, readjusting into place. She noticed the glass of water sitting on the bedside table and reached for it. It was only a matter of moments before it was entirely drained, not a drop left.

"I'm hungry," she noted plaintively, settling the empty glass between her hands in her lap. She blinked, looking dully at her aunt. Her voice sounded strange to her, disembodied, not her own. But she knew that it was and that she was slowly coming back into her own. Each time seemed to take a little less time than the one before, but it felt like a long time until she could come back and everything could fall back into place right away.

"Of course you are, dearie." Marie-Claire set her work in her own lap and looked on at Emalia with indulgent pride, as one would look upon a prize pet. It had always irritated Emalia, whose brow furrowed in annoyance at the pandering. "That's why I've got Catherine down in the kitchens whipping you up a nice apple tart or two to hold you over until dinner. And some tea, of course."

Marie-Claire stood, depositing the knitting on the chair that she previous occupied, and looked dotingly down at Emalia. "Come on, then," she said. "Let's get you up and tidied, and I'll meet you down there, my dear. Be quick about it, though. Anything longer than a quarter hour, and I'll have to send a search party after you."

The portly woman left, leaving Emalia alone for a moment, and her eyes drifted warily toward the window. The faint murmur of conversation and activity in the streets below joined the birdsong, and she sighed. The chill of the place between worlds still clung to her, her hands rubbing her forearms, and part of her wondered if another reason for the cold inside her was the sense of loss. Whenever she came back, it felt like losing just a little part of herself each time. Bit by bit, little by little, and despite the pleasant warmth of the day, she felt cold and lonely.

When she made it downstairs into Aunt Marie-Claire's rustic little kitchen in her rustic little townhouse, Emalia was dressed in a sweater to keep off that chill. She ran a brush through the tangles in her stick-straight hair. She pulled half of it back to keep it out of her eyes and splashed some cold water on her face. It made her feel a little more refreshed, a little more awake, a little more human again as she followed the incredible scent of baking apples and sugar, her stomach rumbling all the way like an incoming storm.

There was a strange man sitting at the kitchen table when Emalia arrived. She blinked in surprise, turning a questioning glance to her aunt, who passed off a nervous sort of smile and a shrug before helping Catherine the housemaid with the tarts. Emalia let her eyes roam suspiciously over the figure sipping tea out of her aunt's best china, sitting in her usual chair, the one facing the bright window over the sink. A young man, though probably at least still a decade older than Emalia herself, dressed very neatly in a smart pinstripe suit. The buttons on his jacket were undone in an air of casualness, revealing a fine silk vest underneath, with a gold chain for a watch tucked into the breast pocket. His chair was angled away from the table to allow him room to sit with one leg cross over his knee, and Emalia could see that the light blue print on his socks matched his tie impeccably. He was incredibly attractive, long and lean with a smooth, blemishless face and sharp green eyes. His dark hair was styled carefully to look disheveled, but in a neat way. He smiled at Emalia, a smooth and cunning expression, and she instantly disliked him.

She realized that he did not simply look young, he looked ageless.

"Who is this?" she asked, wincing as some of the firmness she intended to express came out sounding more petulant than anything.

"Emalia!" Marie-Claire clicked her tongue in disapproval. "Don't be rude. Monsieur Collins is our—"

But Monsieur Collins had lifted a delicate hand to quiet Marie-Claire, setting down his tea cup and administering the use of his napkin before rising to his feet. There was a slight adjustment of his jacket, and he tilted his head as he considered Emalia. She pulled back, finding the gaze too intense for her liking. "Perish the thought,

Madame," he said, with a low, smooth drawl. Even with the warm afternoon, even with her sweater, something about his voice made Emalia shudder as though ice were being trailed down her spine. "The slight in manners is my own, staying seated like that when a lady enters the room. Allow me to introduce myself. My name is Henry David Collins, little lady, named after that great writer and tax evader, Henry David Thoreau. Have you heard of him? No matter if you haven't. You must be Emalia, am I right? Your aunt has told me so much about you." He smiled again, offering out his hand. "It's a right pleasure to be meeting you."

Emalia regarded the hand with suspicion; she felt a strong reluctance to touch this man. Her eyes danced to her aunt, who was glaring with an expression that promised Emalia bloody murder if she even thought of being unkind. So she dutifully took the hand, which was cold and clammy and unpleasant.

"Very nice to meet you, too, Mr. Collins," Emalia responded, her voice hollow as her hand retreated into the sleeve of her sweater, though she really just wanted to wipe the crawling feel of him off on her jeans.

"The pleasure's all mine, I assure you."

"Monsieur Collins will be renting out one of the rooms on the third floor," Marie-Claire explained, waving a large hand over the steam rising up from the tart. "He's on holiday, from the States."

"And excited I am to avail myself to all the charms of France." Not once in the conversation so far had Collins's smile subsided; in fact, the crooked, smarmy thing only proved to intensify Emalia's animosity. "Perhaps you could point out to me some of the highlights of the area, Emalia, with appreciation for a foreigner's sensibility. Your lovely aunt tells me you grew up on my side of the pond yourself."

Emalia's eyes flashed toward her aunt, open to the betrayal she felt inside. Marie-Claire studiously avoided that challenging glare by chiding Catherine on her slicing of the tarts. Emalia looked back to the grinning stranger, knowing there would be no relief from her treacherous aunt, and her resolve and her caution hardened. "I don't suppose she told you why I wound up here, did she?" she asked, her voice laden with sharp venom.

Collins dipped his head as if removing a hat and held his hand to his heart. "Your dearly departed parents, God rest them, were taken off the face of this planet in a tragic accident. My sympathies are with you, Emalia, truly they are. I, too, have long since lost my own parents to…unfortunate circumstances."

"An accident." The words felt dead in Emalia's mouth. "Yeah. I don't exactly like talking about it."

"For that," said Collins, "I can't blame you one bit."

Suddenly heavy with the weight of her loss, Emalia pulled out a kitchen chair from the table and sunk into it, staring at the honey colored wood and the small pink vase bursting with spring flowers. They had always called her parents' death an accident, putting into people's minds the images of bent automobiles, burning buildings, hurricane winds. But their death had been nothing so mundane, and it felt strange to be sitting here, with sunlight streaming in over fresh baked goodies in a kitchen that seemed right out of a home and cottage magazine, while in her dreams, there were other worlds, where things could happen that no one would ever know about. Emalia knew they had been lost out there, somewhere, in the space between worlds, and every time she visited, she searched for them, knowing deep inside it was useless.

If she could, she would go back, right then and there, and search again. But she knew she couldn't, not after just returning from a trip into the further reaches. Dully, she lifted her eyes and saw that Mr. Collins was looking at her, that smile still planted on his face as if it was painted on.

There was something peculiar in his eyes; there was a sharpness there, a deviousness, that didn't match the gentle smile. It was as though the two features belonged on entirely different faces, the smile to someone docile and useless, and the eyes…the eyes belonged to something dangerous and terrible, and Emalia started to have the feeling that she'd seen those eyes before.

Windows to the soul, her mother had called the eyes. That was why, she had said, when we go between worlds, we close our eyes and fall asleep, so that your soul went inward, leaving behind the useless body of the corporeal world. When she was younger, when her parents were still alive, she hadn't completely understood, but that moment, in that kitchen, under the unwavering attention of those eyes, she did. She wanted to close her eyes and retreat away from this world as quickly as she could.

The thud of a plate being set in front of her brought her back, though, followed by that sweet aroma. She picked up her fork and considered the food, another product of a physical world filled with too many heavy things, then looked to her aunt pleadingly. "I'm not hungry anymore," she announced.

"Nonsense!" her aunt scoffed. "You've had such a busy morning, ma petit. It's best you eat up now, or else you'll be famished in an hour and spoil your dinner."

"No," Emalia said, hating the whine that had lifted in her voice, "really, I'm not, and I won't. I would really just like to be excused."

Marie-Claire considered her niece very carefully, then, in a long moment where Emalia channeled every feeling of contempt and desperation and pleading into her eyes, where

Catherine started to feel a bit ill at ease with the pregnant pause, where Mr. Collins just kept grinning, and Emalia could feel it despite looking at her aunt the entire time. Finally, Marie-Claire sighed and nodded her head. "Alright, then," she said. "I suppose the tart will keep in the fridge and make for a nice dessert later. But mark my words, I expect you to finish every last bit of food at your plate come dinner time."

"Yes, ma'am." Without grace, Emalia pushed back her chair and stood from the table, wasting no time in leaving. She muttered a few words about going out and enjoying the lovely day with a book, though she had no intention of doing so. As she headed toward the stairs to return to her room, she heard Mr. Collins addressing her aunt.

"The girl has the right idea," he said. "I must thank you for the treat, Madame, but I'd hate to waste these glorious hours. Much to see and much to do, and not a whole lot of time to do it in. I shall be back after dinner…"

She did not hear the rest of it, bounding up the stairs, taking them in twos, and she almost felt, with her heart leaping into her chest, that the man was actually going to follow her. The idea was absurd, but still, when she got back to her room, she found herself closing the door firmly behind her, turning her back to it and pressing her weight against it as if that would keep him out. She closed her eyes, fighting to catch her breath and wondering how her heart could be pounding so much.

This wouldn't do, of course. If Emalia planned on going back in between worlds, she would have to be calm and collected, or else the resulting trip would be off-kilter and nightmarish. She swallowed air in big, calming gulps, feeling much too hot suddenly in her sweater, almost as if this world was too much for her. Knowing she'd be cold when she returned, Emalia still shucked off her sweater, pulling it over her head and setting it at the bedside table. She considered the empty glass from only a little bit ago, picked it up, and went to fill it from the bathroom sink. She set it down and took a glance around the room, and her eyes danced to the clock.

It was only a matter of time. She had only to wait until the bells tolled again, and she could enter the space between worlds.

One. Two. Three. Four. The last hollow call of the large bronze bells seemed to echo into the distance, and Emalia opened her eyes. All around her, the world was black, speckled with pinpoints like stars, but there were no stars in a place like this. There was almost nothing except for a sharp, bitter cold. Though her breath rose in front of her in the chilly air, Emalia could feel nothing. Her body was still back in the world she had grown up in; she hesitated to ever call it the real world, because the worlds she could find beyond this place were just as real and palpable and incredible as the one she had come from. Here, though, in the space between worlds, there was just as vast nothingness with the promise of worlds, and herself, in the form of her soul, the shape of a great, wide-winged bird with a glittering white tail of feathers. She flapped her wings and propelled her soul-self forward, contemplating where to start her search this time.

She had to be back for dinner; she could not go far, and the next world over was a pleasant place not too different from the world she had grown up in. She had searched it many times, to no avail, but there were beautiful trees and gentle breezes there, a babbling creek and funny, kind animals, and it would soothe her soul to rest there for a moment.

Before she could reach that small pinpoint of a world, though, Emalia realized that she was not alone. She turned, slowed by the nothingness that surrounded her, her glittering form swirling around her like a drop of coloring added to a glass of water. There, near the world she had come from, she saw the serpent. Coiled and sketched in the same glittering white light, it reared its head back and hissed, forked tongue flickering, licking the air.

Emalia almost lost her grip on herself right there, terrified, having never encountered another being in the space between worlds before. And if she disappeared here, then she disappeared from everywhere, she realized, with a new leap in her heart that wedged itself in her long, slender neck.

Despite herself, she let out a call of despair. Is that what happened to her parents, caught and surprised in the space in between worlds so that they were consumed by the nothingness in their ability to retain their selves? The serpent's bright eyes glittered, green and hard, and she realized that she had seen those eyes before.

That's right. The smooth Southern drawl of Mr. Collins filled her head, as the snake unraveled and started to slither forward. Emalia flapped her wings and pushed herself up high, away from the snake, but, in the space between worlds, directions were pointless. She could fly, and he could slither right up after her. She needed to get back to her world, back to the safety of her body, but he was blocking her way whenever she tried. *You've seen me before, in the other worlds, with your parents.*

No. Emalia didn't want to believe it, but she knew that it was true, and her spirit started to weaken. Memories were surfacing out of the nothingness, of her parents teaching her the travel, of a strange friend with green eyes, who Emalia only saw briefly, before that last journey from which her parents never came back.

You look like your mother, the voice continued, and the serpent started to sway, as if dancing to the own melodious timber of his voice. *Back in the world, anyway. Not so much here. She took the form of a cat, sleek and stealthy, but your father, ah, now, his soul was a lot like yours, but fiercer, stronger. He gave me quite some trouble, dug out a good bit of flesh. You're not going to give me that much trouble, now, are you, Emalia?*

You killed them, she realized, feeling weak, feeling almost as though she were fading. She fluttered her wings and she knew, back in Aunt Marie-Claire's quaint cottage bedroom, her eyelids were fluttering too. But she couldn't reach the opening back to that world.

And I intend to kill you, too. I knew it would only be a matter of time before I found you, my dear.

Knowing she had to escape, Emalia started drifting toward another pinpoint, into a different world, any world. It didn't matter now. She knew she'd be safer in the worlds. Kill someone in a world, and you merely kill their body, while their soul can still grow strength in the space between and move into different worlds. Kill the soul in the space in between worlds, though...

She let out a painful howl, something between a scream and screech as she realized that she would never find her parents, not after what Collins had done to them. *Why?* she cried out, pained and desperate and afraid she already knew the answer.

Now, don't get me wrong, sweetheart. The serpent began swirling around underneath her, as if already wrapping her up in his tight bodily embrace. *Your parents were good people, especially your mother. What a beauty, what grace! But you need to understand that me and mine come from a very long line, and this is our turf. We're not used to young upstarts like your parents and yourself slipping on in between the worlds and threatening to mess with the way we like things. We tried to nip this one in the bud, but, well, the little bud got away. No worries, though; just as easy to prune a full bloom as it is the bud.*

The coil tightened and Emalia realized that she could feel every inch of the serpent tighten around her, though they weren't even touching. A trick of the space between worlds, where the space between spirits was just mercurial as anything else. The thought hit her in a frenzy, and she thought perhaps it meant that she really was losing all of her air, but she had nothing to lose. She had to try it, and if he could put the squeeze on her without touching her, perhaps she could reach the opening without really being there.

Emalia projected her energy forward; she spread her wings as if to shove off the invisible hold on her and screeched out in defiance. Her beak went diving toward the body of the serpent with sharp, merciless jabs. Like a cord caught in the wind, the serpent whipped and turned with each blow, emotions of pain vibrating off of him and rippling the nothingness in great waves. She struggled against the fighting creature, but relentlessly went at him until he finally settled and she burst through the opening though it was still a distance away.

The bells were ringing again, and this time, Emalia woke up with a start, a gasp, pitching herself forward and clutching her chest, feeling as though her heart were still being squeezed tight as though in a vice. Sweat beaded her forehead, left her straw-colored hair plastered to her long, slender neck. The birds were still singing outside of her window, and the glass of water sat waiting there on the bedside table, as if nothing had happened at all. Everything was just the same as she'd left it. Nothing had changed.

Except now she knew for a fact that her parents were gone forever, but at least the monster that did was gone, too. There was the strange iron scent of blood in her nose, and, though her heart released, tears released with it, and she sat in her bed, sobbing as she never had before in her life.

The sobs eventually gave way to silent tears, and she looked through watery, reddening eyes out the window, wondering if there was any point to anything anymore. There was a gentle knock at her door and she turned her head, just as it opened a crack and the round, loving face of her aunt peeked in. "Emalia, ma petit, come have your dinner."

Emalia threw back the covers and rushed forward, throwing her arms around Marie-Claire's bulk and hugging her as tightly as she could, until she remembered the hold of the serpent and loosened her embrace. Though she couldn't imagine her aunt would have any idea of what just happened, she felt sympathy radiating off of the woman, as she gently patted the girl's back until she settled. "Come now, let's get you all fed, shall we?"

Quietly, sniffling back more tears, Emalia followed Marie-Claire down into the dining room, but a horrible feeling crept over her that had her pausing before the door. "Auntie?" she asked, her voice so quiet she couldn't be sure Marie-Claire even heard her.

"Yes, Emalia?"

"Mr. Collins, is he—"

"Joining you for dinner after all?" Sending an instant dagger of fear into her, a familiar voice drifted in from the living room, and Emalia cautiously stood looking in at the neat suit, the suggestion of messy hair, and the green eyes glittering over at her from the head of the table. He smiled, and, this time, it matched his eyes. "Turns out there was no rush on all my other things after all, my dear, no rush at all. It seems I have all the time in the world. The game isn't over yet."

No, Emalia thought to herself, resisting the urge to close her eyes, and, instead, channeled her strength in her tightened fist at her side. It isn't. Not by a long shot.

Afterword

The volume preceding the afterword is a collection of seventeen stories, some of which were written within the year of their publications, others of which go further back, to nearly a decade ago, when I first started scribbling down words in the form of shorter fiction. Many of them dealt with the topics of youth and transformation; these, which include *Dragon Rising, Flesh and Feathers, Spider and Fly, Kanoa*, and *The Space Between Worlds*, were all stories penned for a contest run by Morgan Dragonwillow, and have won a spot in my heart.

The Wartburg Incident (often subtitled "Martin Luther Throws Things") came about in a college class, during a life-changing moment when a narrator on a video about the Reformation elaborated for two seconds on a historical footnote about a stain on the wall of Wartburg Castle, from when Martin Luther allegedly threw his ink jar at the devil. Some of the best stories have and will come from historical footnotes like this, and this is why I always read the footnotes, too.

The Truth and Lies of a Body in the Snow and *Swing* were both stories I have previously published on my Elfwood page, many years ago. The former of which was even graced with a Moderator's Choice, which was the penultimate of acheivements for me at that time.

Jolene earns a great deal of debt to the Cake song of the same title; hopefully, many fans of the band will notice even more of their work referenced throughout. One day, I hope it will be a part of a bigger project involving many stories inspired by various Cake songs. *Just Right* is also another story I hope to develop into a larger project, as well, taking us even further into the depths of Dr. Wilhelm Grimm's Institution for the Criminally Insane.

Black Stones would have likely never been finished if it weren't for the urgings of C. Michael Hubbard, while *Lilacs* and *Purgatory* are two stories that may have never found a home if I hadn't gone ahead and made one for them myself.

Bibliophile has also been previous published in Central Michigan University's Fiction Collective publication, *10;29*, while *9 September 1976* and *Bridge Over the River Yuanfen* appeared in the CMU graduate studies publication *Temenos* under different names in the Spring of 2009. I was reading a lot of Da Chen and Dai Sijie when I wrote those two pieces of flash fiction and I still consider them two of my favorites.

Thank you for taking the time to read a few of the tales I have to tell. I hope you enjoyed reading them as much as I enjoyed creating them, and here's to looking forward to many more to come.